The Blue Moon Pact

Nix Belmont

Contents

CHAPTER 1

"Which do you think is better? The blue or green?" Addie asked, lifting up two dresses to her body in the mirror. The light from morning sun making her olive skin glow.

I leaned back against her headboard and analysed both options. The green dress was flowy with a low back and ended just below her knees. It was held up by two thin straps that would make it easier to slip out of.

The blue one, however, was long with full length sleeves cuffed on the ends. It had a v neckline that ended at her sternum. There was also a slit from mid-thigh to the floor. With the deep blue colour and the amount of thigh showing it was definitely the sexier of the two. Our parents probably wouldn't be too thrilled about it. But that is honestly just a bonus.

"The blue one. Suits the theme of today's celebration," I replied. "It's also guaranteed to catch the attention of that husband-to-be of yours. Maybe even get you celebrating the perks of being alive on the day of the dead." I wiggled my eyebrows and she scowled at me.

She cursed, stalking into her closet but I caught the flutter of her heartbeat. She was wound tight. Unlike all the previous Blue Moon Festivals this one was also celebrating the union between her and Ryker Belmont. A union that would join our packs. It was a big deal.

"What are you going to wear?" Addie asked from the closet.

I flicked through her chemistry textbook on her bed. I didn't understand a single thing especially not her scribbles. "I have a few options in mind. But don't worry I'll make sure not to embarrass you in front of Belmont."

Truthfully, I didn't have a clue what to wear. Hasn't been much of a priority for me. I don't even think that I have anything that my mum would approve of for tonight.

My phone buzzed next to my hand. Drawing attention away from my sister's babbling. A series of messages from Robin.

Robin: Pierce

Robin: Pierce come on!

Me: What?

Robin: You up?

Me: Obviously. What do you want?

Robin: I need my hardrive. Urgently. I left it in your car.

Robin: Can you bring it?

Robin: Pleeeeeease!

Me: Ugh. Fine

"I'm gonna go," I called out. Addie pooped her head around the door. "Robin needs me to drop something off and I have to pick up a few things from town for tonight."

"Want me to get you anything?" I asked as I walked out the door.

"Like what?"

"Condoms." I ducked just before her shoe hit me in the head. It bounced of the wall, and I ran out laughing.

My fingers skimmed over the spines of the books while I silently read the titles. None had caught my eye. But as I looked through the shelves, tucked behind another book was a black hardbound book with gold vine foiling. I ran my hand over the bevelled cover, feeling all the grooves and sharp edges.

I opened it to the front page where it read Liber Animarum in scrawled ink. As I flipped over the book my finger sliced on the edge of the page. Before I could stop it, my blood streaked on the bottom drying instantly to the page.

"Crap," I muttered. Robin's going to be pissed. I continued flipping the pages taking mere glances at the content. The book seemed to be an encyclopedia or something of weird, occult things. Unfortunately, not my type of book. Despite how pretty the outside was.

Not wanting to buy the book I hid it behind one of the self-help books on the bottom shelf. Suddenly, the light above me stuttered and flashed before turning off. Taking that as my signal I made my way towards the front of the store.

At the cashier till, Robin fiddled with a pile of books scanning and placing them in boxes. Today she was dressed in a simple black shirt and jeans with her blue lanyard hanging from around her neck. Her vibrant red hair was piled high on her head with a few curly wisps framing her small face.

"Find anything?" she asked without looking up.

"No," I replied. "But your light in the fiction section has gone out."

She tipped her head back and sighed. "It's been doing that all week. I literally replaced the bulb yesterday. Probably some fault in the electricity."

"I can ask Ethan if he'll stop by and check. Better yet, you could ask him. I'm sure he'll say yes." She scowled at me, but her cheeks tinged with a light pink. I refrained from pointing it out though.

I tilted my head and took a strand of her hair into my fingers. "Did you redo these?"

"Yeah. Thought it would be nice to refresh my colour for tonight." Robin was naturally a red head and proud of it, but ever since high school she's been dying her hair different shades of red. This time it was a fire truck version of her natural colour.

"Looks good."

"Speaking of tonight, how's Addie doing?"

"Nervous, obviously. This will be the first time in over a century our pack and the Belmont pack have been in the same territory without trying to kill each other. I think if no one gets killed it will be a success."

The Belmont and Parsons packs have been enemies for years. It originally started over land and developed into hating each other purely because. But with the rise of vampire clans and hunter groups, the Alpha's thought it would be a good idea to unite our packs. Which is how sweet Addie got engaged to the bastard, Ryker Belmont.

"Well, I would be nervous too if I had to marry Ryker Belmont. The man is dangerous and word on the street is he has a temper."

I had heard those rumours as well which is why I've never met their family. When my dad told me about the agreement and who Addie was marrying, I flipped out and Addie had a panic attack. I was planning on killing him at the first meeting. Had the whole thing planned out. Unfortunately, mum caught on to my plan and they all decided I was not to go near the Belmont's. Probably for the best, I guess.

Over the months it seems Addie's come to terms with it. In fact, I might even go as far as saying she liked the man. But I won't know for certain until tonight when I meet him for the first time.

"I have a feeling tonight is going to be interesting," Robin commented. I nodded my agreement.

I couldn't help but feel that tonight would either end in a celebration or in blood. And I am perfectly fine with either.

Chapter 2

I closed my eyes and held in the groan threatening to slip out. Ahead of me at the exit to the parking lot were two women arguing. To the side of them one car had hit the parking gate riding slightly on the pole. The second car had t-boned the back of the first. The crash wasn't bad and both cars only have slight dents.

Tapping my fingers on the steering wheel I tried to concentrate on my playlist which was currently blasting Gravity Glidin by Masked Wolf. Unfortunately, I could still hear the blonde over my music. She was going off about how the other lady was making her late for something important and how she almost destroyed all her precious items. Most of which seemed to be books and candles, based on what was peeking out of her boot.

Right at that moment I wanted to get out and drag both women. Toss them to the side. Maybe gag them as well.

My phone buzzed from the console drawing my attention away from my violent thoughts. I picked up without looking at the caller I.D, something I would regret doing.

"Hello?"

"What's up, princess?" Ethan greeted.

"Bloody hell," I groaned. I was not in the mood to deal with his crap right now.

"Ouch, princess. It really hurts when you act like you're not all for me." I rolled my eyes at his smug tone. I wish it hurt.

"What do you want Ethan?" I asked impatiently. Before he responds, the women finally move on and I have to refrain from sighing in relief. I didn't need to give Ethan anything more to annoy me with.

"I need you to pick up the cakes from Willow's bakery."

"Why can't you?"

"The elders want us to double up the security around the forest before tonight. You know, don't want some random human to stumble upon a hundred or so wolf shifters running through the forest. Would be pretty disastrous."

Despite being an hour and a bit from the town centre every now and then hikers, tourists or just dumb townie's come up to our territories. We haven't had a human attack in a long time but with tensions running high, and that many wolves running on primal instincts, you can't be too careful.

"Well, you're lucky you got me before I left town."

"Wonderful! Knew I could count on you."

"Prick," I said after he hung up.

Willow's bakery was near the town centre and was the best cake shops we had. Upon entering the bakery, I noted the exposed wood and vines that climbed across and hung just below the beams. There were a few tables and chairs situated around the room, most filled with customers.

"Hi there! How can I help you today?" the chirpy woman asked as I approached the counter. She smiled up at me and I couldn't help but smile back at the woman. Her name tag attached to her black apron telling me her name was Elaine.

"I'm here to pick up an order for Parsons," I replied. She tapped the screen for a bit, long enough for me to catch sight of her necklace.

Around her neck was a simple chain holding a snake with a crescent shaped gemstone in the head. It was a clear quartz gem. To almost anyone else it would seem like a perfectly normal necklace, but Robin had told me about witch talismans. A witch typically had a crystal embedded in an animal that represented their power and chosen familiar. Robin said that under natural lights you can see the magic swirling beneath.

I'd only been in the bakery a handful of times in my life, but the Willow's Bakery has been part of the town for decades. As far as I knew though, it was a human establishment. In fact, a witch hasn't been sited around here for years. Typically, they avoid shifters as much as possible.

"Yes, I have your order back here. Just give me a second." The witch went to the back, and it gave me a little time to take in my surroundings. Nothing stood out that said this was a witch establishment and as I pulled in the scents around me all I got was baked goods, humans and wolves.

Elaine came back out followed by a taller woman whose face was obscured by the large white box. I didn't even need to see her necklace to know she was a witch. Power was practically radiating off her and it set shivers down my spine.

They placed the large cake box and five shorter boxes on the counter. With the box out of her hands the other witch turned towards me and gave me a small smile. The freckles littering her nose and cheeks standing out against her pale skin making the light brown of her eyes stand out. Despite what I was sensing, nothing in me felt alarmed by either one.

"Do you want any help taking these out to your car?" the freckled witch asked. I considered denying her request but there were a lot of boxes and I only had two hands.

I accepted her help and we walked out to my car parked a few spaces from the shop entry. She carried the smaller boxes while I carried the main box. We piled the food into the back seats as my boot held the rest of my shopping from today. Some clothes, bird food for Nero and some weapons that I haven't put away yet.

"Thanks for your help, uh..."

"Penny." She held her slender arm out to me, and I grasped her fingers. There was a slight tingling sensation when our skin touched, but she pulled her hand back before I could think anything of it.

"Pierce," I offered back. I glanced at her necklace that fell out from under her white apron. It was a bird with wings outstretched and a red stone in the centre. A ruby by the looks of it.

"Well, it was nice to meet you Pierce."

On the drive home I couldn't help but feel a little restless. I put it down to nerves, but deep down I knew that wasn't it.

Chapter 3

"Pierce!" I flinched from the high pitch of my mum's voice. "Why aren't you ready?"

Turning, I took my mother's appearance in noting her chosen outfit for the night. She was wearing a simple black boho styled dress that flowed around her making it look as though she was floating. She had slicked back her white hair and under the lights of the clearing, her blue eyes seemed to glow. Although right now a storm was brewing, and it was aimed directly at me.

My eyes roamed over my blue jeans and white shirt. Looking back at my mum I shrugged. "I'm gonna change after I finish setting up."

"No." She grabbed my arm in a vice grip and began dragging me across the clearing. "You need to change now. The others will make sure the place is ready."

"Okay. Okay," I dragged my arm out from her iron grip. She turned on me and despite my towering form, I took a step back.

Glancing around she lowered her voice so only I could hear her and said, "You will also be on your best behaviour tonight because so help me, Pierce Joanna Parsons, if you start something up with the Belmont pack after all we've done and achieved, we'll be honouring you in the next blue moon ceremony. Understood?"

I resisted the urge to roll my eyes. She'd been panicky all week. Control yourself, Pierce. This is an important day, Pierce. Do not mess this meeting up, Pierce. Honestly, you would think I was planning a mass bombing with how she had been acting. "I understand, mother."

Once I reached the house – escorted by my mother no less, I reluctantly made my way to my room. Slamming the door shut the walls shook and by extension Nero's large silver cage. He flapped his wings aggressively at me, squawking his displeasure.

"Sorry, Nero." Unclipping the latch, Nero wasted no time bursting through the cage to fly around the large expanse of my room. Satisfied with his slight freedom he perched himself on my vanity. Making no indication that he's cared he was close to tipping over all my items.

Lying on top of my navy blanket was two dresses, both similar in style but different in colour. One was a deep purple with an almost burgundy colour while the other was simple black. On most days I wear black so going purple would be a nice change. But you know what they say about comfort.

I pulled the black dress over my head and the back ending just below my shoulder blades showing off part of my raven tattoo that stretched across my back. I gave myself a once over in the mirror. The dress was simple and plain, curving around my breasts. It cinched at my waist before flowing past my knees.

"What makeup look should I do?" I asked Nero, but he just ignored me. "Simple it is."

Foregoing a full face of foundation, I spot concealed, adding a bit of bronzer around my already tanned face and applying the smallest amount of blush to the high points of my cheek. Not satisfied with just mascara and brown liner I took a deep brown and slightly smoked out the eyeliner adding more depth to my brown eyes. To finish the look, I slipped on black flats and brushed through my hair. The layers from the wolf cut I had gotten earlier this week framed my face.

As I stared into the mirror my irises seemed to change colour shifting from a light brown to a dark almost black colour. But when I moved closer to the mirror the colour in my eyes seemed to bleed into the whites turning them completely black.

Gasping, I moved back but a skeletal hand reached out of the mirror and wrapped itself around my face pulling me into the mirror. Darkness wrapped around me as I fell seemingly without end. Until I was grabbed mid-air. The sudden change in speed sent shockwaves of pain shooting through my shoulder and for a horrible second, I thought my arm was about to be ripped off.

But I almost wished it did as a rotting face peaked out of the darkness. I screamed and thrashed against it, breaking its grip and falling only to be grabbed once more. I continued to scream as more hands wrapped around me, pulling me under the darkness.

Their bony bodies crawled over me, grabbing each limb and stretching my skin. Their broken voices rattled around my skull. "Join us. Join us. Join us," they repeated until their voices drowned out my own.

They tugged. They bit and there was nothing I could do but suffer as they tore flesh from bone. As they slowly morphed me until I looked just like them.

I shouted in pain falling to my hardwood floors with a thud. Frantically, I looked around seeking any glimpses of the creatures, but I was met with my empty room. I clutched my chest and silently rocked back and forth whispering to myself that it was okay. I was safe. I was in my room, and I was safe. Yet, I couldn't shake the feeling that I wasn't.

I wiped the tears that began to fall but winced when my fingers grazed my cheek. Pulling my fingers back I noted the blood. That's when my ears cleared, and I heard Nero squawking madly. Grabbing my phone from my bed I flipped the camera on and saw three surface-level scratches across my cheek. Thankfully they were already healing.

Harsh banging on my door had my heart leaping in my throat, but it was Addie's voice that called out. "Pierce! Come on! We're going to be late, and you know mum and dad will flip. Get out!"

Taking a couple of deep breaths, I calmed my nerves. Running my fingers through Nero's soft black feathers I reminded myself that it was a dream. It had to be.

"Thank you." I gave Nero a peck on the head, grabbed my bag and rushed out of my room.

Waiting for me at the front door was Addie dressed in the blue dress I had suggested she wear for her future husband. Despite the blood rushing in my ears, I couldn't help the grin that spread across my face. One that grew exponentially as I noted how much care she took in her makeup considering she hated wearing it.

"Shut up," she muttered, a pink flush coating her cheeks and I couldn't hold the laugh in as we walked out of the house. The horrible dream already beginning to fade into my subconscious.

Chapter 4

The air was cool, raising goosebumps along my exposed skin. We had gathered around Lake Isla where we had honoured our dead every blue moon for the last century. Except this year we were joined by the pack we had considered our enemies for most of the century.

The lake was five minutes out from the house and everywhere you looked a wolf was standing in their human form. The heads of both packs stood just off the wooden deck. A few meters separated us.

I scanned the people that had come and were it not for the fact that I knew everyone in my pack, you wouldn't be able to separate the two packs. Everyone was wearing loose-fitting clothes that would be easy to remove to shift. The Belmont men all wore unbuttoned shirts with pants that hung on their hips. It was difficult not to ogle their defined bodies, but I reminded myself that they were Belmont's and arseholes.

Addie's arm brushed against mine a silent command to pay attention. Standing before everyone was the Alpha's of the Belmont pack – Alpha Dane and his wife Alpha Mary. They were talking about something. Behind them stood my parents – Alpha Thomas and Alpha Helen.

It was a little hypocritical of Addie to tell me to pay attention when she was sneaking glances at Ryker whenever she could. An action that wasn't lost on Sammy who was standing next to her. Based on the tenseness of his body he was getting annoyed with it.

Like me, Sammy didn't like the idea of Addie marrying Ryker. Unlike me, he was able to keep his temper in check.

"I want to thank you all for joining us this night and want to extend a warm welcome to the members of the Belmont pack here with us," my dad's voice boomed. "As Alpha Dane mentioned, tonight is a special night for both packs as we celebrate the union of Ryker Belmont and Addison Parsons. A union we all hope will remain strong through the times." A few cheers and whoops sounded throughout.

I tuned out the rest of the speech having heard it a million times. Tonight, was the remembrance for the thousands of wolves that died a thousand years ago on the first night of the blue moon cycle. A genocide that wiped out hundreds of packs and is the reason why there aren't that many packs around the world despite the slowly increasing population. In fact, most believe that the only reason we gain more power and strength on this night is the dead's revenge for what happened to them and to ensure it never happened again.

Once the speech was over, we were all invited to lay a rose in the water as our way of honouring them. Every pack has their own way, but this was ours. Soon the surface of the lake was freckled with roses floating under the soft blue glow of the rising moon. Most were red in colour, but some were black signifying the recent loss of a wolf. Addie had placed a black one for a close friend of hers that had died in a hunt overseas.

Once the final rose was laid silence washed over the area. Anticipation buzzed in the air as we all watched and waited for the moon to hit its peak. Waiting for the rush of power that we get only on the first night of a blue moon, making us some of the most powerful creatures on this earth.

I cast a quick glance towards the Belmonts only to find Ryker staring at my sister with a heated looked. Sensing my gaze, he turned his grey eyes to me and for a moment we stared at each other, neither breaking eye contact. Out of respect for his rank, I should have lowered my eyes, but I wanted him to know that I didn't care about his power and position.

I also couldn't deny that a part of me wanted him to feel a little insulted and maybe start something. Not that I would win. But it would make things interesting. Yet, a little voice in the back of my head reminded me that while I still didn't like his pack, he didn't seem to be a threat to Addie. In fact, she seemed to really like him, and so for that reason, and that reason alone, I turned my eyes away.

With a minute away from the moon being in position, I could feel my wolf scratching the surface. But a familiar squawk drew my attention away. Looking into the trees I caught sight of a raven with a gold cuff around his foot.

What was Nero doing here? I thought I had locked him back up in his cage. But then I remembered the terrifying dream and realised that I left without locking him back up.

His beady eyes were trained on me as he flapped his wings rapidly. My eyebrows scrunched. He squawked again and I surveyed my surroundings not seeing anything that would cause alarm.

Turning back to Nero I flashed my eyes, signalling for him to take flight, but the stubborn bird stayed put flapping his wings again.

Before I could try and decipher his warning, a rush of power coursed through me. My wolf surged to the surface the moment the moon hit its apex, demanding to be set free. It took a lot to hold it back. Around me, everyone broke out in celebration and without hesitation, people stripped and shifted into their wolf forms. Howls filled the night air.

Behind me, Addie had shifted into her timber-coloured wolf. She pranced towards Ryker's much larger black wolf and rubbed her head under his chin. It was disgusting honestly.

Looking around most had already shifted and taken off into the night. But I noticed that Logan Belmont hadn't yet. Catching my eye, he flipped me off before shifting into his large greyish-brown wolf. Rolling my eyes, I felt for my wolf. I couldn't wait to teach that smug moron a lesson.

I went to call the shift when Nero let out another squawk. I'm going to kill this bird, I thought angrily. I looked at the stupid bird and he began aggressively flapping his wings and squawking again. Taking flight only to loop back to the tree.

A wet snout pushed against my shoulder, and I met the blue eyes of a light grey wolf. My mum snapped her jaw at me, and I didn't need to hear her to know she was telling me to hurry up. I resisted the urge to roll my eyes.

I glanced once more at Nero planning the bird's funeral when he swooped towards the lake. He flew around in circles over the water squawking non-stop.

Confused, I slowly walked towards the edge looking over the water trying to pinpoint what he was seeing. Crouching on the soles of my feet I hovered slightly over the water. At first, all I saw was my reflection, but slowly my face seemed to hollow out and darken. I inched closer to the water.

Deja-vu hit me like a truck. I really should have recognised the similarities between this and the dream because just as the feeling hit a hand shot out from under the surface.

Chapter 5

My body was ripped backwards but not before sharp bony fingers wrapped themselves around my face. I landed on my back groaning from the blunt force. A large wolf hovered over my face its light brown eyes peering down at me. Before I knew what was happening it opened its mouth and dived for my face. But instead of biting me, it dislodged something from my face, spitting it out to the side.

I looked down to see a skeletal hand twitching in the grass. With a yell, I launched to my feet and looked to the water where another bony hand gripped the wood. Then the impossible happened.

A corpse slowly pulled itself onto the dock decking, its handless arm flaying about. I couldn't believe what I was seeing. It wasn't possible. Its hollowed skull twisted to face me, and it opened its jaw. I clamped my hand around my ears as it let out a high-pitched scream.

For a moment I was frozen. Images of the corpses reaching for me from the darkness only to tear at my skin flashed in my mind. My lungs constricted as my heart pounded. I was stuck in a moment of terror not being able to do anything but stare at the creature before me.

From behind, warning howls rang through the air snapping me back to reality. To my horror corpses both skeletal and slowly decomposing waded out of the lake. A foul rotting stench wafted from them made worse by my heightened sense of smell.

The corpse that had grabbed me launched itself at me. Before I could react, the wolf sprinted past me meeting the creature mid-run. The greyish wolf ripped the skull clean off. The bones fell to the ground instantly.

The wolf looked back at me with a feral grin, and I didn't need to see his human form to recognise him.

Logan Belmont.

I was saved by Logan Belmont. Talk about ironic.

All around wolves launched into battle with these creatures. Some clearly enjoying the battle more than others. Sammy being one of them. His dark grey wolf moved from one corpse to the next. He was in clear competition with a few of the others.

Above me, Nero squawked again. It was all the warning I got. I jumped out of reach of a small body that had crawled its way to me. Lifting my foot, I struck down hard on the skull shattering it into tiny pieces.

Behind me, a cry as a creature latched itself to a wolf biting down on their shoulder. I whipped my hand out, grabbed the spine and pulled. Without hesitation, I snatched the skull off and crushed it in my hand.

I turned to the wolf who had shifted back to his human form. He wasn't one of ours. Crimson streamed from the deep bite mark on his shoulder. Kneeling, I grabbed his shoulder and wiped some of the blood.

"It's not healing," I whispered as I watched the wound ooze. His healing should have kicked in by now but there was no indication that it had.

"I can't shift," the young boy – a teenager if I had to guess – whimpered.

"What?"

"I can't shift. I can't shift. I can't shift," he repeated over and over. His body shook as tears rolled over his freckles.

"Okay, okay. It's okay," I comforted. I lifted his head and forced his teary eyes to look at me. "You're gonna be perfectly fine alright. We're gonna fix this. But right now, I need your help. Can you do that? Can you help me?" He gave a short nod.

I pointed across the trees towards another wolf that had shifted back to her human form laying naked on the ground. "I need you to take the injured wolves and take them to the house. I need you to protect them." His lips quivered but he steeled himself. Straightening his back, he bowed his head and took off towards the female.

Truthfully, I had no idea if he was going to be okay. I have never heard of something striping a shifter's ability to shift. It was unheard of. Although everything that had happened so far was unheard of.

I glanced around the chaos. Furry forms sprinting around with a few wolves in human form. My gaze snagged on a fiery red wolf standing protectively over a couple of smaller wolves and a small form lying in the grass. A rotted corpse running towards her.

Leaping from my position, I called my wolf forward. Mid-air, my body vibrated and transformed into the deep brown fur of my wolf form. Landing on all fours centimetres from the creature, I snapped my jaw out, ripping its head off.

I moved to the next creature. Spitting out the rotted flesh that got caught in my teeth. It took everything in me to not gag and vomit from the foul stench and taste that stained my tongue.

Pierce! Don't let them bite you! Robin's voice yelled in my head.

I moved my body out of the way just as a skeletal creature grazed my shoulder. It shot past and towards Robin. She crouched and then pounced, meeting the creature mid-air.

When she landed the body had been shredded, bones falling around her.

I walked up beside her and brushed my body next to hers.

Go to the house, I commanded the two younger wolves. And take her with you. Robin nudged them on with her snout.

Around us, things seemed to be slowing down. Not many corpses left.

We helped those we could and by the time we got rid of the last of the creatures we were exhausted. The extra power faded the closer we got to sunrise.

As we trotted towards the house, Sammy's voice boomed through my head, Addison!

But we were too late. Just a few feet away I watched as my sister got dragged into the lake.

Chapter 6

I didn't think. Didn't even hesitate before I dived into the cool water. My fur absorbed the water and weighed my body down making it easier to paddle toward her. Addie had shifted. Her body flailed as she fought against the creature dragging her deeper towards the bottom.

When I got within an arm's length I pushed my wolf back, forcing my shift into my human form. As my fur receded the water grew freezing, and my limbs threatened to lock up. But I pushed through it. Adrenaline pumped through my system keeping me in motion.

Upon seeing me, Addie's brown eyes widened in both fear and relief. Her hand stretched towards my own. Our fingertips grazed. But something heavy latched onto my back and began pulling me away from her.

White-hot pain shot through my body as the creature bit into my neck piercing skin. Water rushed into my mouth as I attempted to scream in pain. I twisted my body seeking to dislodge the creature, but it sunk its teeth deeper. With the lack of oxygen, my lungs burned. I honestly didn't think my situation could get worse and then a firm grip wrapped around my leg.

Each time they bit through my flesh it felt like I was being set alight. My head filled with the screams that I couldn't voice. Agony tearing at all parts of me.

This is it. I'm going to die. I'm going to die. I'm going to die.

Despite the blinding pain and blurred vision, I could still see Addie. My beautiful older sister floating, suspended in the dark water. While the light of the moon barely penetrated where we were I could see her clear as day. And to my relief, not a single thing grabbed at her.

This was it. I was going to die. But at least there was a chance that Addie would survive.

When the burning in my lungs was too much, I opened my mouth once more inviting the water. My lungs filled and soon I just floated further under the surface. The pain became a dull thud. The darkness around swallowing the noise in my head and cries of my body.

There was nothing. Just me floating towards the embrace of death.

Maybe it was minutes, hours or maybe it had only been mere seconds. My eyes flew open as a torrent of water rushed out of my mouth. My body was roughly turned to the side as more water spewed out.

"That's it. Get it out. Come on, Pierce," a soft voice spoke in my ear. It was hard to discern anything around me. My vision was blurred, and everything sounded muffled. I gasped, struggling to breathe without feeling like my lungs were burning.

Far away from me - or maybe it was right next to me - deep voices spoke in harsh tones. Nothing discernible. Slowly, my vision cleared, and I pulled myself into an upright position. Kneeling over me was my mum, her face pinched in concern as she held my face.

"Addie," I croaked. She looked to the side and there Addie was wrapped in the arms of Ryker who was in a heated argument with Sammy.

I tried to stand up but almost fell on my back had it not been for my mum's firm grip on my upper arms. Giving her a small smile, I leaned on her for support and stood to my full height.

"Pierce!" Addie yelled. I stared in shock as my small framed sister pushed Ryker away from her and dodged his attempts at grabbing her again. She ran to me, the white dress shirt fluttering around her thighs. I didn't have much time to tighten my hold on the jacket that barely covered my butt before Addie had wrapped herself around me.

I was slightly bigger than her both in height and stature but with how she was holding me, you probably couldn't see the difference.

"Are you okay?" she asked against my hair.

"In a bit of pain with the way you're holding me," I wheezed.

"Oh, sorry." She pulled back but didn't let go. Her eyes glistened with unshed tears.

"You're not healing," Sammy said as he came up to me, giving me a concerned once over. The wounds in my neck and legs burned. As though to prove his point a drop of blood leaked out and dripped down my chest.

"None of them are," Robin said from behind me. We all turned to her. She gave me a sympathetic glance before looking to my dad. "Please call an emergency meeting. There's something I need to tell all of you."

CHAPTER 7

There had only been a few times in my life when I've been in my dad's office. The most recent time was when we got told Addie was marrying Ryker. I broke the wooden desk which he had replaced with a darker and much sturdier one.

Dad leaned against the window arms crossed. His strips of grey hair stark against his dark strands. Mum sat in his office chair while the rest of us were scattered around the room. It was silent as we all mulled over Robin's information. Well, her theories.

Addie shifted on the couch clearing her throat. "So, what you're saying is someone has cursed our pack which has resulted in the dead rising from the lake - which, concerningly, is a lot, and unless we somehow break this curse they will rise again and attack us until we're all dead."

"Basically," Robin said. She stood by the desk, her hands behind her back. I gave her a small smile trying to give her a little comfort.

"This is ridiculous," Sammy muttered. My mum gave him a sharp look. "What? Everyone knows she's off her rocker." Logan snorted which earned a look from Alpha Mary and both men received a glare from me.

"I know it's hard to believe -" Robin started.

"You're talking about necromancy. A practice that hasn't been wielded by witches in over a century. It's not hard to believe. It's ridiculous," Alpha Dane stated. I internally shivered at the mention of the black magic.

"Not to mention there haven't been any witches in these parts for decades. Especially not ones with the power and skill to wield that kind of magic. Magic that the High Council of Witches monitors closely." Disappointment dripped from my dad's words.

Robin cast her eyes down and anger surfaced in me. I hated how they treated her as though she was crazy or an idiot. Yes, Robin loved being in her head and she revelled in how different she was to everyone else. That was how she was raised. But she was also kind, caring, empathetic and incredibly well-read in the history and lore of different cultures and species. In fact, she was probably more intelligent than most in this room.

"How do we know if we've been cursed?" I asked ignoring everyone else in the room. Robin's eyes lifted to meet mine and I could see the relief at knowing someone was taking her seriously.

"Pierce -" my dad started.

I ignored him and looked pointedly at Robin. "We'd need a witch. I don't think this is something that can be broken without one. Maybe we can contact the witch council?" Growls of displeasure were all the answers we needed to know that wasn't an option.

"The witch council wouldn't help us unless there was something in it for them. No, we will handle this ourselves." My dad's words were final. But given they were stupid; I wasn't going to let it rest at that.

Before anyone could say anything more, I stood and levelled them all with a look. "We just got attacked by skeletons and rotting corpses. Creatures whose bite has rendered many of our pack, including me, without the ability to shift. So, I couldn't give a flying rat's ass whether or not any of you believe we're cursed. Robin knows what she's talking about and unless you have any other explanations for what just happened, none of you gets to say anything."

In retrospect, it may not have been the best idea to blow up and yell at all the top-ranked wolves in the packs, but given how tired and in pain I was, I didn't give a shit. Everyone was silent. My dad's angry gaze seared into the side of my face. But I refused to meet his eyes.

Alpha Dane stood but Alpha Mary grabbed his hand and in a firm voice said, "Pierce is right. No matter how impossible Robin's theory may seem, something bad and clearly magical is happening and getting help from a witch would be the smartest course of action."

Alpha Dane looked as though he was going to argue but decided against it. There were a few grumbles around the room, but no one spoke up against her.

With that settled all we had to do was find a witch to reverse this whole thing before they came back. No pressure at all.

I stared into the mirror. The same one that showed me the terrifying vision of last night. Brown eyes stared back at me illuminated by the streams of the early morning sun. That familiar spark no longer visible.

Instead, they were dull.

Searching for something.

Begging for anything to happen.

Yet no matter how long I stared. No matter how many times I called the shift, my signature amber never flashed. My teeth never sharpened. My claws never extended.

I slammed my hand against the mirror shattering it into little pieces that scattered over my sink and tiles. From outside the bathroom door, Nero squawked and flew around the bedroom.

Tears rolled over my cheeks pooling into the sink. I was so caught up in my feelings that I hadn't heard the door open. Only when the person moved behind me did I register their calm presence.

"I can't feel it," I whispered. Soft hands wrapped around my shoulders, turning me. Gently, my face was tilted up and I stared into the soft blue eyes of my mother. "I can't feel my wolf."

She pulled me into a hug, and I let the tears fall. I didn't know what to do. It felt like someone had ripped a part of me out. Just an empty void where something should be.

Without my ability to shift was I even a shifter? Without my wolf, was I even me?

I didn't know and I was too afraid to ask the question out loud. So instead, I just cried in my mother's arms.

We stayed this way for a bit before someone banged on my bedroom door calling her away.

Once she left, I changed into my comfort clothes. Nero tucked himself into my neck as I lay curled on my bed. Both of us watched as sunlight filtered into the room. It was a small action. One that we have frequently done through the years. Yet, at that moment it meant everything to me.

As sleep grabbed at the corner of my mind one thought played over and over: finding a witch that would fix all our problems. Good news for me because I knew exactly where to find one.

CHAPTER 8

My fingers tapped the table in time with the music playing in the background of the café. Every now and then I would glance at the clock, groaning every time it ticked closer to the three. On a normal day, I could be considered impatient. But today, I was on a whole other level.

My phone buzzed for the fourth time in an hour and as with all the other times I ignored it.

All I wanted was to go back to the compound and prepare for the possibility that Robin was right and those things were coming back. Instead, I was sat on the window seat of a café waiting for a witch that may or may not have something to do with what happened last night.

Sure, I probably could tell my family what I was doing. In fact, I'm sure they had a better plan than mine, but I didn't do that. No, I left the moment I woke up saying I wanted to get some things from town. Not a total lie.

I gulped down part of my third coffee relishing the way it burned down my throat. A piece from my second chocolate muffin followed suit. The caffeine and sugar caused a slight buzz in my system which did nothing for the anxiety building while I waited for Penny to show. Yes, this was a little stalkery. She had taken her lunch break when I arrived and apparently hers are over an hour long.

The sky overhead darkened, and I had to remind myself that we still had a few hours until dark. Still, as I watched a variety of people walk through the bakery's door, there was no Penny. I was growing impatient.

"You know, if you're that desperate for cake, you could just walk in and buy one instead of glaring at the door."

I closed my eyes and released a heavy sigh. "Logan," I greeted through clenched teeth.

He stood a few paces from me, hands in his denim jacket pockets. His taupe hair was curlier today. The messiness making him seem younger almost boyish. He wasn't. He was a nightmare.

With a stupid grin, he plopped himself in the chair across from me, partially blocking my view of the bakery.

"What do I owe this unpleasant visit?" I asked in a monotonous tone.

"Just wanted to see how the little Parsons princess was doing after last night." I bristled at the nickname just as he reached over and took a piece of my muffin. "So, are you going to tell me why you're staking out the bakery instead of helping your pack?"

"I am helping the pack, prick." I took another sip and focused on the warmth of the liquid instead of the infuriating male in front of me. Who was still blocking my view.

"And how are you doing that? Last I checked cakes don't kill the dead." Then he dropped his voice and leaned in. "Are you trying to eat your feelings away?"

I almost whipped the cup at him. Instead, it cracked under the pressure of my fingers. Instead of giving him a reply, I focused back on the bakery just as Penny in her white chef's jacket and high bun went sauntering into the bakery.

Knocking back the remnants of my coffee I grabbed my jacket and left. I didn't make it far outside the café before Logan gripped my elbow to spin me around. He threw me off balance and I had to steady myself with a hand on his chest. His very hard chest.

"What the hell are you doing?" I yelled.

"What are you?" he fired back. "Why are you after that woman?"

"It's not your concern." He lifted his thick eyebrow. Knowing he wasn't going to let this go and I only had a limited window, I dragged him into a little alleyway.

"She's a witch," I said.

His eyes widened. "Are you sure?" I nodded.

"Her and another one of her co-workers were wearing those necklaces that represent their familiars. I sensed their magic when I stopped by to pick up the cakes yesterday."

"Why didn't you say anything when you found out or this morning at the meeting?"

"It honestly slipped my mind, and I didn't remember it until I woke up." He gave me a look. Not entirely true but it was all he was getting.

He was silent. Then he asked, "Do you think either one is powerful enough to do something like this?"

I thought on it for a moment and remembered the power that radiated off Penny when I met her. "Penny, the one that we just saw, was practically radiating with power when I met her. She could have done it."

"And what if you're wrong and she had nothing to do with what happened?" I rolled my eyes. But Logan grabbed my arm and forced me to look at him. "I'm serious Pierce. Witches are extremely sensitive about this stuff. You accuse her of being a necromancer without proof and this could end even worse for you, or our packs."

This close to him I could see the specks of gold in his eyes and how his pupils dilated every now and then. I hated it.

Pulling away from him I replied, "I'm well aware of the risk of pissing off a witch. But right now, this is our only option. Now you can either stay here with your tail tucked between your legs or you can help me deal with the witch. Which will it be, kitty?"

Logan snarled. He hated the name more than I hated being called princess. I loved it.

He thought about my offer and then cursed under his breath. I grinned as he stepped to the side allowing me past. Falling a step behind me we made our way to the bakery.

Chapter 9

"Well, can't say this is how I saw this going." I rolled my eyes at Logan's dry tone.

My arms were crossed as I stared at the struggling witch. Penny was sitting on the wooden floor of the small storage room. It was barely able to fit all three of us. Especially when she began thrashing about, kicking her legs wildly.

I sighed as she screamed behind her makeshift gag. Yeah, this was not how this was supposed to go. But we had very limited options. I had to roll with it.

"Penny," I said softly, hoping she would calm down. "I know you're scared, but I'm not going to hurt you." Logan scoffed under his breath. I glared at him and took a step toward Penny. She whimpered and pushed herself as far back as the shelves would allow.

"I don't think she believes you," Logan mused. He leaned against the door, eyes glinting with humour.

Ignoring him, I tried again. "I know you're scared, and honestly if we had more time, I would have done this completely differently. But we don't." She looked at me like I was crazy. Maybe I was.

"Last night my pack was attacked by dead people who crawled out of the lake. Now, last I checked, we didn't have a zombie apocalypse. So that leaves being cursed by a witch as the only other option." Penny stopped moving. Her eyebrows drew together. "Given that you and your co-worker, Elaine, are the only witches in town, you're at the top of our suspect list."

Staring daggers, she mumbled behind her gag. Ignoring it, I continued, "When I touched you yesterday, you zapped me." Then I asked the all important question, "Did you curse my pack?"

Penny closed her eyes. Head bowed. I moved closer and that's when I saw her necklace. It was glowing red. The bonds tying her hands snapped. Pulling off the gag she flung her hands toward me and yelled, "Perdere!" (destroy).

The room filled with a blinding light and magic exploded through the room slamming into me like a truck. We were blasted through the door, slamming into the wall with force. Debris from the roof and walls fell, burying us.

I opened my eyes, blinking away the blurred vision. My ears rang from the sudden explosion and for a moment I couldn't remember where I was. But then it all came screaming back.

I was still as I processed what just happened. That explosion should have killed me, or I should at least be seriously injured from the roof collapsing. Yet I was here, alive and with minimal damage by the feel of it.

Confused, I pushed a piece of the wall that had fallen on top of me to the side and that's when I felt the tightness around my stomach. Looking down I saw muscled arms wrapped around me in a vice grip. I followed them around to Logan whose eyes were closed. My body cradled against his broad chest. Not only had he covered me with his body, but he had twisted us so he received the worst of the impact.

I twisted around to face him, and his arms loosened. His head lolled to the side and a thin stream of blood ran from the top of his head and down his smooth cheek.

"Logan," I called as I shook his shoulders. But there was no response. I leaned my head against his hard chest and listened intently. When I heard the steady thumping of his heart I sighed in relief.

Cupping his head, I gave him a once over. Further down his body, a large piece of wood was lodged in his side.

"Shit. Logan!" I yelled again. He was out cold. As long as that piece was in his body, he wouldn't be able to heal properly. So, I wrapped my hand around the thick piece. Saying a silent prayer, I ripped it out. That woke him up.

He cried out in pain and pushed me away. His eyes snapped open and instead of his usual brown eyes, they were golden.

I breathed out in relief. His wolf was near the surface which meant his healing was kicking in.

Looking around, the bakery was destroyed. The walls had been decimated and there was a clear view of the front where the windows had been shattered. Under a few pieces of rubble, I could make out a few people. From the sounds and slight movements, no one seemed to be dead. Which was a relief.

Behind me, someone coughed, and I tensed. Turning, I saw Penny stagger out of what was left of the storage room. My vision went red, and before I realised what I was doing, I grabbed her by the throat and slammed her into the ground.

"You're fucking dead," I spat. My fists were raised and ready to pound into her face.

In a panic, she wrapped her hand around mine and my head snapped back. A slew of images flashed before my eyes: Corpses forcing their way out of the ground; bodies piled in the streets; water running red.

I pushed out of her grip and staggered backwards. Shaking my head to disperse the last of the images, I was stunned into silence. Penny rolled over onto her elbows, coughing.

"I didn't curse your pack," she wheezed through deep breaths.

"What the hell was that?" I demanded.

"That's what I saw when I touched you. I swear I didn't curse you or your pack. We had nothing to do with what happened last night." Her teary eyes looked at me, pleading for me to believe her.

"You're a witch. You could have made those images up." She shook her head rapidly. "When I met you, I sensed your power. I bet you're powerful enough to do something like this."

"No, I'm not. Necromancy is forbidden. Anyone found practising is put to death." She pulled herself up on wobbly legs. "Besides, my family are nature witches. We've never dealt in the dead. Our magic is the complete opposite of necromancy. I swear."

I scoffed, "Last I heard, nature witches couldn't explode a building."

Logan coughed and groaned drawing my attention away from the witch. I knelt by his side. He tried to pull himself up but cried out in pain. "Stop moving, you idiot. You're still healing." I pressed him down onto his back causing him to wince.

His eyes flicked to Penny who stood over my shoulder and a growl emanated from his chest. "I'm going to kill you," he snarled.

I shoved my head in front of him. "Calm down. If you kill the witch, she can't help us."

Penny knelt by my side and looked at Logan with guilt. "I am so sorry. I know you probably don't believe me, but I had nothing to do with what happened to your pack. Neither did my cousin." Then she levelled me with a determined look. "But I can help you save them."

Chapter 10

I glanced at the clock. Ten past five. My phone, tossed from one hand to the other as I paced around the room. This was taking too long. We needed to be back and preferably with a solution.

"You know, pacing around like that isn't going to make any of this go faster," Penny said while typing away on her phone. I scowled at the witch. But I decided to take a seat next to her.

"Well, do you have anything?"

"Not yet. He's doing some tests."

"Great."

I leaned my head against the wall and watched the long hand of the clock tick by each minute. It was excruciating. Nothing about this day had gone to plan and it was safe to say that it was just going to get even worse by nightfall.

Robin had texted me earlier, said the pack was under lock-down and that a few members of the Belmont pack were coming to help just in case. I laughed at that. They didn't believe there would be another attack, yet here they were bringing in reinforcements.

I was kind of surprised they stayed. I half expected the Belmont's to be gone by the morning, but they weren't. Instead, they were out helping those injured and were now prepping for the inevitable. Something which I should be doing as well instead of sitting on my ass.

But what use would you be? Without my ability to shift I was basically human. A wave of sadness washed over me. I blinked back the sudden tears that sprang forth. I wasn't going to cry. Especially not in front of the witch.

Five more minutes went past when Elaine – Penny's cousin – walked through the door that led into her office-like space. Penny said she would be able to heal Logan and help us with our little issue. Which was why we were currently in her living room.

"Is he okay?" I asked shooting to my feet. Behind her, I caught a glimpse of Logan pulling his shirt over his head. His back muscles were taut with scratches that were almost completely healed.

Elaine nodded. "He'll be fine. I applied a herbal salve that should speed up his healing. Not that he needs it, being a wolf and all." She muttered the last part more to herself than anyone else and eyed me warily. I wanted to snap back saying I wasn't a wolf, but I held my tongue.

"So, you think your pack is cursed huh?" Elaine stated more than asked, crossing her arms. I suddenly felt like I was about to be reprimanded by my mother.

I opened my mouth to respond, but Penny interrupted. "Results are back. There was nothing in your blood. He also asked around to see if there was any talk about a necromancer in the area, but there was nothing."

I rubbed a hand down my face. Back to square one.

"Are you positive what attacked you were corpses and not some...magical creature maybe?" Elaine asked.

"They were skeletons. Some were even still in the decomposing process. What else could they possibly be?"

Elaine studied the floor. Quiet with thought. "We need to check if your pack or your land has been cursed. The fact that it happened only last night means it would have to be something introduced into your pack recently." Like another pack, but I didn't say that. Truth be told a lot has changed in recent months. It would be like finding a needle in a haystack.

"We'll need access to your lands," Elaine said. I tensed. Most hadn't seen a witch before and there was no question of the welcome they would get. But if this was the only way to save the pack, then they would have to suck it up.

"How long would your testing take?"

"Using the power from the blue moon, it wouldn't take me long. The more powerful the curse the easier it will be to find.

Once we can identify the curse, we can break it, and all of this will be over." *One can only hope.*

I pulled my phone out and sent a quick message to Addie telling her that I found a witch that could help us, but I needed her to ask dad for permission to let me bring them to pack lands. He probably wouldn't be happy with it, but Addie always managed to get her way. She would get me permission.

"What if it isn't a curse?" Penny asked.

Elaine was silent and when I looked up, she had a troubled look. "If it isn't a curse then that leaves necromancy. If there is a necromancer in town, then we're all in trouble. Not just the wolves."

My phone vibrated and I looked to see Addie had texted back.

"Well, guess we'll find out tonight. I was just given permission to let you two on our lands."

I crossed my fingers and prayed that this was an easy fix. But then again, when is it ever?

Chapter 11

It was silent as we pulled up outside the house. The only people we had seen so far were the patrols. Almost everyone else was either at their own homes or the main house. Addie had told me the meeting was going to be at our house though. Not only did it avoid even more panic, but our house was also a five-minute walk from the lake. Ground zero of this whole thing.

Ethan sauntered out of the house with Lance - one of the Belmont enforcers - in tow. I looked Logan over with his blood-stained clothes and then glanced at the two witches in the back seat. They were both tense and looked around in alarm. Couldn't blame them.

I got out of the car and Logan followed suit. The witches stayed in the car at my command. We met the two part way and I was silently thankful that Logan's visible wounds had healed. Lance tensed looking Logan up and down.

"What the hell happened to you?" Lance growled. His eyes darted between the two of us. I probably didn't look much better than him.

"Pierce," Ethan growled in warning.

"There was an explosion in town. But we're both fine," Logan answered.

Ethan looked at me and then they flicked to the witches still in the car. "Did it have something to do with them?"

"No. We weren't near them when the explosion went off." The lie rolled off my tongue with ease. I couldn't tell them that Penny tried to kill me. She would be severed into tiny little pieces before I finished the sentence and without my wolf, I couldn't protect them.

"Where did you find them?"

"They were in town and noticed them yesterday." I left out that they worked at Willow's Bakery.

"And you didn't think to tell anyone that?" Lance scoffed. Ethan growled a warning at the enforcer.

"I was preoccupied with other things. Besides, it's not like witches haven't gone in and out of town before." I shrugged and held Ethan's stare. He knew I was leaving things out, but he wasn't going to push, especially in front of the Belmonts. But I had no doubt that he would let Sammy know.

"Let's get this over and done with," Ethan said.

With a sharp nod, the cousins got out of the car and walked toward us slowly. Elain looked towards Logan who gave her one of his disarming smiles. It was a trick. One he perfected years ago to hide the danger lurking under. But it worked and Elaine seemed to relax a bit.

Suddenly, Penny stopped walking. She looked around, scanning the surroundings.

"What's wrong?" I asked.

Her brows scrunched. "I don't know. There's...something."

We all looked around as well but there was nothing. Maybe she was just nervous and paranoid. Or maybe she was sensing the curse.

From above, a sharp squawk sounded. In the sky once more was Nero. I watched as he flew above the trees and then doubled back, his squawking becoming more urgent. Adrenaline coursed through my veins, and I eyed the trees he flew over.

"Penny!" Elaine called. Their necklaces glowed in unison. Elaine's was white while Penny's was red.

"They're here!" I yelled just as the first howl sounded.

Everyone jumped into action. All three men shifted into their wolf forms. Behind us, more people rushed around shifting into their wolves until the forest was filled with the sounds of violence once again.

I grabbed Penny and Elaine and we raced to the house just as corpses broke through the tree line. Logan's wolf form jumped in between us and the creature, severing its head from its body.

We made it to the house piling through the door. Nero swooped in after Elaine, narrowly missing my head.

On the floor in the living room, Addie was wrapped in a large jacket while Ryker was crouched over her. His eyes glowed bright gold. I didn't need my sense of smell to know what they were doing before the attack.

Ryker gave Addie a look before bounding through the door. Nero perched himself on the table that had been moved to the side. Clearly to make room for Addie's extracurricular activities.

"Well, at least one of us was having fun today," I remarked as I positioned myself in front of the window. I couldn't see anything, but I could hear the fighting.

"Shut up," Addie said. "And you are?"

"This is Penny and Elaine. They're the witches I found," I answered for them without looking back.

"Well, nice to meet the two of you."

"I thought they only came out at night," I stated, recalling what Robin had said earlier. "The sun hasn't even fully set yet." As if to prove my point, a stream of dusk light streamed across the front garden.

"Where's the rest of the family?" I asked, realising I hadn't seen any of them yet.

Addie adjusted the jacket around herself as she came up to stand next to me. "Mum and Alpha Mary went to the main house. They're trying to abate the panic. At least twelve wolves were bit last night and can't shift. The rest were out patrolling. They were on their way here."

"I'm sorry, what is this about you not being able to shift?" Elaine interrupted. She had wrapped her arms around herself and seemed a little paler than moments ago.

Addie looked at me and I nodded my head. "We found out that any wolf that got bit by those...things, couldn't shift anymore. They couldn't even feel their wolf."

"I'm one of them," I added.

"Why didn't you tell us this before?" Penny asked. Her necklace was glowing brightly. A lot more than her cousin's.

"I didn't think it was that important." I shrugged. I didn't add that I felt it was humiliating and I was pretty sure I would break down if I told them. I was barely keeping it together as it is.

"It's incredibly important!" Penny yelled. Addie bristled at her tone.

"Oh shit," Elaine muttered and fell into the couch. She dropped her head into her hands and began rapidly breathing. Was she having a panic attack?

Pulling herself together she lifted her head and gave me a sombre look. "Your pack isn't cursed." Well, that's a relief. At least I thought it was.

"If they're not cursed..." Penny let her words hang in the air.

If we weren't cursed, then that left only one other option.

The cousins shared a look before Penny said, "Call the council."

Chapter 12

E laine was in the other room making some calls. Apparently, the council wasn't as easy to contact as one might hope. Unless of course, you violate one of their rules. Then you can never get rid of them. At least that's Penny's opinion of them. Clearly, she isn't a fan of them.

Addie had left to help at the main house and send word about the new development.

Necromancy.

If you had told me yesterday morning that I would be battling the walking dead, wolf-less and alongside a witch whose family has been secretly part of this town for decades, I would have laughed and thought you belonged in a looney bin. I mean, these are the kind of things that you see in movies or hear in legends.

I looked out the window and watched as a couple of wolves – unknown to me, bound through the trees chasing a corpse. Envy reared its ugly head at the sight. Suddenly, I became very aware of the empty feeling swirling inside ready to bring me to my knees.

Minus the undead situation, tonight would have been a perfect run. Weaving in and out of the trees. Basking under the light of the blue moon. Even with the potential for death, I would have gladly gone out hunting and fighting until they killed me.

Light footsteps sounded behind me drawing me from my thoughts. Without turning, I asked, "Anything?"

With a sigh, Penny stood beside me watching as the moon began its ascent above the clouds. "No. You would think that a necromancer bringing the dead to life to terrorise a town would be enough to get direct communication, but no." Her words dripped with bitterness.

"Why do you hate them so much?" I asked curiously.

"Because they're useless and never do anything to actually better the witch community." Her arms were crossed. Venom coating her words.

I raised a brow at her tone. She sighed. "My family hasn't had the best...experience with the council." At my confusion, she continued, "I spent most of my childhood with my dad's family in America. They were constantly fighting with the council. But even then, the council never really helped witches. Ironic I know given my aunt works closely with the council."

"Well, Elaine says they're the only way to help," I said cautiously. Penny stood quietly. The silence saying what she wasn't.

"Elaine believes they're good and they're what protects us from the bad. And maybe some are. But that's not what I've experienced."

"But they're the only ones who can help...right?"

She looked at me and under the light of the moon, her brown eyes held a slight iridescent glow. She dropped her voice before replying, "The council will stop the necromancer, that is without question. The question is whether they will stop them before your pack ends up dead."

Dread filled my stomach. The only chance we had was the council. I hoped Penny was wrong.

The wind was cool against my skin. A stench of death hung in the air. My back was pressed up against the brick exterior of the house as I scanned the trees. There was no sight of movement and nothing but the soft howling of the wind to fill the night.

Nero shifted his weight on my shoulder before taking flight. His wings beat against the wind as he flew over the grounds and towards the trees. It took a few moments before he looped back giving me a single caw.

I moved towards my car with speed, relying on my senses to alert me of incoming danger. With my keys in my hand, I move to the boot of my car and unlock it. Piled in the back was a few bags of bird food that I may have forgotten to take out. Not that Nero would have eaten it anyway. Picky creature.

To the side was a pile of jackets and books. Moving the items, I unlocked the padlock to the small compartment. In most cars, this is where you keep your spare tire or tools. Not mine. No, I had guns, knives and boxes of ammunition. I may have also picked up a few grenades. Grabbing one of the bags, I filled it with all my weapons.

Heading back, I reached the bottom step when the wind changed direction. A strong overpowering scent of decay hit me in the nose. I jumped backwards just as a large, rotted hand reaches for me. In front of me stood a large corpse with half his head peeling off to reveal the cream bone.

I flipped onto my feet and dodged its advance. Despite its size, it moved fast. Almost too fast for me to dodge. With each missed strike the creature growled. Which was an anomaly given its lack of throat.

I feign to the right and when the creature followed, I step towards its left and threw an uppercut. My fist connected with the underside of its skull and cracked the bone. Fleshy pieces fly off revealing even more of its hideous underneath. Pain spiders down my hand and I fear that I may have broken my knuckles. But I moved on.

It stabled itself and launched towards me. I planted my feet and when it got within the vicinity, I dipped and twisted my body. I kicked my foot up and pushed all my strength into my thighs, kicking its skull clean off.

Another corpse broke through the tree line and sprinted toward me. Nero dived from the sky and latched his talons onto its skull. I scurried to my bag and pulled out the shotgun, loading it before taking aim.

"Nero!" Nero released the thrashing corpse only for me to pull the trigger. The bullet splintered and tore its skull into different pieces.

I grabbed the bag and bolted into the house, closing it when Nero flew in.

"Are you okay?" Penny asked.

I gave a short nod and dropped the bag onto the table. "Please tell me you have good news."

"Elaine said the council has sent someone." I groaned in relief. Finally, this will all be over.

"How long until they're here?"

She hesitated. "Tomorrow."

"What?" I yelled. "There's like ten hours until sunrise. We can't wait that long!"

"She's trying to get them to come sooner but the witches that deal with this kind of thing are busy. The closest one can only get here in the morning."

Busy. They're busy.

Anger surfaced and without thinking I grabbed the edge of the coffee table and turned it over sending my bag full of weapons crashing into the wall. Bending to my knees, I held my face and tried to calm the rage coursing through my veins.

We would barely survive this night.

My breathing became laboured, and my hands burned to grab anything and release the pent up violence.

"Your pack will survive this night. They're strong," Penny consoled. "But I won't lie to you. Even if the witch comes, it could take a little bit before they can detain the necromancer."

I lifted my head and watched as the witch picked up a handgun that fell out of the bag. Red swam in my vision.

"But there is another option," She turned to me and offered the gun. I waited for her to continue. "We deal with this ourselves. We find the necromancer."

"And then what? We can't do anything until that fucking witch shows up!"

"The dead aren't being raised by a curse. They're being raised by a spell, one that relies on a constant connection to a power source. Given that they appeared before the moon even rose, the witch is drawing from their own power."

"So?"

"So...if the spell relies on the connection to the witch all we would have to do is break the connection." The corners of her lips quirked up. "Kill the witch and the connection breaks. Kill the witch, and we save your pack."

CHAPTER 13

I clutched the shotgun to my chest, aiming the nozzle to the ground. Without my wolf sight and the trees blocking most of the light from the moon, it was difficult to see more than five feet in front of me. The extra gun and ammunition attached to my side were my only comfort.

Each shift in the shadows and rustle of the bushes urged my feet to move faster. I was close to the lake. Even blindfolded I knew the way to the lake. I spent my entire life in these woods and knew it like the back of my hand.

Behind me, a branch snapped. My heart beat wildly. I crouched behind a tree and whipped my head around. It was hard to see anything. I took a deep and steadying breath hoping to centre myself. Listening past the wind, I picked up on faint footsteps getting closer. The crunch of leaves underfoot signalling their location. When they were a few steps away I cocked the gun and jumped out.

"It's me! It's me! Don't shoot!" Penny screamed, hands flail-
ing in the air. Her pale skin bright against the backdrop of the
dark forest.

I cursed under my breath and lowered the gun. "What the
hell are you doing?" I whisper-yelled. "I could have shot you!"

"Yeah, I can see that," she said in a shaky voice. She pushed
the stray hairs away from her face and straightened.

"Well?" I asked impatiently.

"Oh, I realised the spell might go better if we did it at the
lake with an unobstructed line to the moon." Was she serious?
I wanted to tell her she was being stupid and risking our lives
for something that could have been easily and safely done at
the house. But the stench of death started getting stronger.
Instead, I grabbed her arm and pulled her towards the lake.

After practically dragging Penny stumbling through the
trees, we made it to the lake. From what I could see there was
no danger. But human eyes could be easily fooled. Along the
edges of the lake were drag marks and kicked up dirt. But I
couldn't tell if they were from a few minutes ago or from last
night.

I closed my eyes and listened to our surroundings, sifting
through what was nature and what was danger. Satisfied that
there wasn't any immediate danger, we made our way to the
dock. My grip, tight on the handle of my shotgun.

At the edge of the dock, Penny kneeled and laid out a map of the town. She then placed four candles representing the four elements in the four directions.

"Can you fill this jar with water?" She handed me a clear jar and I hesitantly filled it keeping an eye on any changes in the lake's surface.

"How long will this take?"

"It shouldn't take long, but I've never had to locate someone as powerful as this. I've also never had to do it under the pressure of the dead potentially killing me."

She sprinkled a dark powder into the water turning it into an opaque red colour. With a flick of her wrist, she lit the candles. Pouring a circle of the liquid around the map she sat on her heels and closed her eyes. Her necklace began to glow as she muttered the spell.

I hated this. We were wide open. Open for an attack on all sides.

The wind began to pick up creating a symphony with the rustling of leaves. A few howls sounded but they seemed a bit distant. My hand twitched as I focused on every shadow and every ripple that the lake water made. The moving trees made my paranoia even worse.

Penny's auburn hair flowed around her and for a moment I was struck by how ethereal she seemed to be. The moonlight cast a white glow while her necklace and the flames from the candles coloured her in reds and oranges. She almost looked like the embodiment of fire.

Her chanting grew louder, and the flames grew bigger. On the map, the liquid spread out like veins and slowly connected making thicker lines. A circle.

A high-pitched screech emanated piercing my eardrum. To my horror, a bony hand punched through the dirt and dragged its body from under the ground. I pointed the gun and fired straight through its skull. Behind me, there was a splash. At the end of the dock, a corpse was dragging itself up and over the wood. I fired again but there was only a click.

"Shit." I palmed the barrel and swung on it, hitting its head off like T-Ball. I reloaded the gun just as another broke the surface. "Penny, hurry up!"

I was firing and reloading, but they kept rising through the water and out the ground. We were going to be overrun very soon.

How many bodies were in this bloody lake?

I was running out of shotgun ammo and soon would be relying on my pistols. Then, my fear became reality. Two creatures came bursting from the trees straight for us.

"Penny!" I kicked out at the corpse that tried to grab my leg and shot at the two barrelling towards us. The first was shot down, but I missed the second. It was too fast for me to reload.

It leapt and landed on top of me. The only thing stopping it from biting me was the shotgun which it was trying to gnaw through. I lifted my knee and used my hip to flip the creature over. Taking position above it I brought the butt of the gun down on its skull. Over and over. Bashing it in until the skull turned into little shards.

I stalked towards Penny, readying to rip her up, location or not. But when I got closer, I noticed her necklace. The stone swirled with a violent red. The liquid on the map writhing and crawling towards her open palms. I reached out to her but when my fingers grazed her jacket she snapped back, and she looked at me with milky white eyes.

"Run," she whispered and then the flames of the candle burst high, blasting me backwards.

CHAPTER 14

T he ringing in my ears drowned out everything around me. Dizzy from the blast, it took a while for my vision to recover. But when it does my stomach catches in my throat.

Fire burned along the dock scorching all in its wake. Penny was still on her knees but streams of dark red cascaded from her nose. Her face contorted in silent agony. The fire was inching its way closer to her and if I didn't do anything about it, she was going to burn.

I pushed off from the ground and sprinted toward her. Fire licked up my arms as I reached out and wrapped my body around her. Ignoring the burning sensation, I tackled her, and we dived into the water. She thrashed for a few seconds before going limp in my arms. I pushed us to the surface and her head lolled.

Securing her in my one arm, I began to swim to the shore. But her body grew heavy and then recoiled out of my arm.

I dived in after her and watched as a corpse dragged her further into the depths.

I propelled forward and wrapped my hand around hers. The lake itself was cold but Penny's hand was even colder. I tugged her toward me while it tugged her back. Stuck in a constant tug-of-war. I didn't know how long a person could survive unconscious and underwater. But I couldn't have the only witch that could help me die.

I tugged again and then latched my other hand on the corpse. Like a wave crashing over me, my head snapped back, and my vision filled with black.

Coldness, like death, spread throughout my body. Fear consumed me. I couldn't see or hear or even feel anything outside my body. Not even the water that I had been submerged into.

Who are you? A voice whispered, echoing all around me. I spun in place. At least I think I did. I couldn't tell.

Who's there? I called out. Except it didn't feel like I said the words.

What are you? Not human. Not a witch. It hummed in contemplation. Something brushed along my cheek.

There is something... It trailed off. An overwhelming feeling of malice snaked its way over my body, constricting my lungs.

What is this? Why can't I move? Why can't I see?

Panic rose in my chest. I tried to move. Tried to scream, but there was nothing.

My body seemed to float in this void, and I could feel myself growing weaker by the second. A finger lightly scraped against my brain and pure terror washed over me. He was everywhere, yet nowhere. He was in my brain, and I didn't know how to get him out.

I need to get out. I need to get out now.

Help! Someone, help me!

The stranger chuckled darkly. No one can help you here. You have been marked. Your soul, mine. His laugh bounced around my head.

You're dying, he sang. Soon to be mine to play with. How nice!

No. No. No. Please, God, not like this. I don't want to die like this.

But then I saw it. A tiny glowing spark – no larger than a pea, floating in front of me. It called to me. In desperation to leave whatever this was, I reached out and grazed it with my finger.

A painful shock travelled up my arm. My vision burst with colours, chasing away the darkness but not before I heard the maniacally laugh. Around me, images flashed of graves, churches, corpses, crying people, dead animals and the ringing of church bells.

I launched up coughing violently, water pouring out of my open mouth. The burning in my lungs and throat is a feeling I will never get used to and hope will never have to feel again.

"Shit, Pierce, are you okay?" Logan was kneeling in front of me, his gold eyes scanning my body.

I hit his hand away and scowled at him. "I'm fine, Belmont."

Penny was on her side coughing up water as well. Elaine was holding her, her hands pressed on her back and chest. Her crystal glowed as she muttered under her breath.

I stood on shaky legs and Logan had his arms out readying to catch me. Something I would have cussed him out for if I wasn't distracted by the fact that he was bare-ass naked. I turned my head and hoped that he hadn't seen my cheeks flush. Although, he could probably hear how my heart skipped a few beats.

"Is she okay?" I asked.

Elaine looked up at me and glanced away when she saw Logan behind me. "I'm fine," Penny gasped. She waved Elaine off and tried to get to her feet. But almost fell to the ground had I not gripped her elbows.

Once she stabilised herself, she gave me a tap of reassurance. "What the hell were you thinking?" Elaine scolded. "You know how dangerous it can be to do a locator spell without the proper protection! You may as well have used a megaphone telling them that we're onto them. They could disappear and the council may never catch them!"

"And what the hell were you thinking doing the spell out here and not in the safety of the house?" Elaine threw her hands up in exasperation. Her eyes, wide with fear for her cousin.

"I thought I could get a better, more precise location on her."

"Penny-"

"It didn't go exactly how I thought, but it worked. Kind of."

"You know where the witch is?" Logan asked. His eyes sparked.

Penny grimaced. "The spell sent me into her mind." Elaine opened her mouth, but Penny silenced her with a hand. "I don't know where she is exactly, but I got glimpses of where she might be and what she's doing."

"And?" Elaine pushed.

"And if we don't stop her tonight, no one in this town will survive the next twenty-four hours."

Chapter 15

"**S**hit," my dad muttered. Shit was an understatement. In fact, it was the king of understatements for this situation. Silence descended on the room as we all took in the information.

When Penny jumped into the necromancer's head, she found out that she was able to draw power from those bitten. And she got a shit-ton from the first attack. Every time one of us was bitten, our life force was drained and powered her up. Anyone else would have died instantly. But apparently, it was different for shifters because we had two life forces - ours and our animals. While we could survive one bite, the second would kill us instantly.

"If she manages to kill everyone in town and harness their power, there is no telling what horrors she would release on the country. She's power hungry and won't stop until someone puts her down," Penny finished talking and then took a seat by her cousin.

Learning that we were just the beginning and that it would only get even worse, was a hard pill to swallow. Suddenly, the stakes became even greater. It was no longer about trying to just save the pack but potentially the whole country. At the very least our town.

Things had quietened outside. It was disturbing. The corpses had just dropped where they stood. One second they were animate, the next a pile of bones. We were pretty certain it had something to do with the locator spell Penny did. Maybe it spooked her. It was doubtful that this was going to last very long, but we took it as the chance to regroup.

Outside smoke billowed through the air. Invisible against the black sky but the smell was strong. When the bodies dropped, people didn't waste any time to begin disassembling them. Most were crushing the bones into as fine a dust as they could get. But some were burning them.

"Is there a way to reverse what she's already done?" Sammy asked, glancing at me.

"I don't know," Elaine responded honestly. "What she's done is unheard of and honestly, before today I would have said impossible. I've never heard of anyone animating the dead and then using them as a way to syphon power. It's way beyond my knowledge."

I leaned against the wall. My arms crossed over my body. Addie stood next to me and being so close to her gave me the strength to not slide down the wall and tune everything out.

"How many have been bitten?" my dad asked.

"Eighteen, including those from tonight's attack," my mum responded. Addie sucked in a breath. Eighteen wolves meant close to half of our pack was now human.

"Anyone that's been bitten needs to be put in the main house along with our other vulnerable," my dad said.

"We can bring in more wolves," Ryker said. "The Morelli pack will also aid us should we need it."

"You'll need it," Penny said. "She's panicking now that she knows a witch is helping you. She'll throw everything at you. At this town."

"Maybe she wouldn't be if you had waited for me instead of jumping into her head," Elaine remarked.

"I didn't jump into her head on purpose," Penny defended. "It just happened."

Outside the window, Nero was sitting on the lower branch of the tree staring at me. As I stared into his beady eyes, my mind drifted, tuning out the others.

Why us? What did we do to deserve this? As though in answer, Nero flapped his wings sharply. He was right. Nothing. We didn't do anything to deserve this.

While no words passed between us, it was almost like we could understand each other. As though he could read my mind and I his. I silently chuckled. I'm going insane if I suddenly think Nero understood anything beyond the basics that birds knew.

It's been a long two days.

Something that Penny had said earlier was bothering me. She had mentioned that something drew the necromancer to town, but she didn't know what. That our pack wasn't targeted until after the first attack. Elaine had added that something here must have been a beacon for the spell which is why the attack started here instead of down at the town cemetery. The obvious choice.

We all thought that maybe it was the stronger life forces or that we were supernaturals. But that didn't feel right. As I stared into Nero's black pupils, the memory of the creepy voice telling me that I was marked rose. But how was I marked? Was I marked at birth? No. No, there's something else. How does he connect to this? What am I missing?

I sifted through the days leading up to the festival. Was it the joining of the packs? No. We weren't cursed. Penny's friend and Elaine checked that. Was it the witches? Did the necromancer sense Penny's power and seek to get it? No, she wasn't anywhere near here on the first attack. Maybe it was how we...

The book.

The bloody book.

Nero's wings flapped faster as I recalled my trip to Robin's bookstore. I found a book that I thought was about cults and weird, witchy stuff. When I touched it, I had felt a tingly sensation that I had just brushed off as static. But what if it was magic that I felt, like when I met Penny.

I pulled out my phone and fired off rapid texts to Robin.

Me: Robin!

Me: Where did you get the book that had all those weird symbols inside?

Robin: What?

Robin: What book?

Me: It looked kind of culty or witchy.

Robin: There's an entire section dedicated to witchy, occult stuff. Be more specific.

Damn it. Think, Pierce. Maybe I was wrong, and the book was just a book. But my gut was telling me, that wasn't the case.

I need to get that book. Even if it didn't have anything to do with the necromancer, perhaps Elaine or Penny could use it to help us. Then, an idea dawned.

Me: Did you sell any books yesterday?

Robin: Really?

Robin: You're asking me about sales right now?

Me: Just answer.

Robin: Yeah, a bunch. Why?

Me: Was any of those a witchy book?

Robin: Yeah. One.

My heart sped up.

Me: Describe the book and the person that bought it.

She took a little bit to respond, but when her reply came through, I wanted to reach into the screen and kiss her. Instead of writing a response, she sent me the security footage of the sale.

Me: I COULD KISS YOU!

Robin: I take payment in the form of vodka.

Me: Done.

I watched the footage and low-and-behold a woman was buying the book that I had touched. Thankfully, Robin's boss had installed good quality cameras that gave a clear view of features. Including the clear features of the woman that I was almost one hundred per cent certain was our necromancer.

Just as the video ended, Robin sent another text with the words, we're going to see Moulin Rouge after this, attached to another video. This one was me reading the book and gave a nice shot of a few of the pages I flicked to. I would gladly see that play with her a hundred times over as a thank you.

"Penny. You said in your glimpses you saw a book. Did it look like this?" I showed her the zoomed-up image, interrupting whatever discussion or argument they were having.

"Yes, that's the book. Where did you get this image from?"

I zoomed out and showed a closeup of the woman's face. "It was a book at Robin's bookstore. This is the woman that bought it."

"I don't recognise her," Elaine said. Her brows crinkled in concentration.

"Who cares," Addie said. "What's the book?"

"A grimoire by the look of it," Penny answered.

"Wait." I flicked to the video of me and zoomed in on one of the pages that had a diagram of some kind.

Elaine looked over the video and seemed troubled. But when Penny looked, she visibly paled. Fear oozed out of her eyes. She clutched her necklace and muttered what sounded like a prayer.

It wasn't a prayer.

Chapter 16

The house shook and the wall behind Penny began to crack. Dust cascaded down. Random cracks spider-webbed from the bottom to the top. No. Not random. The cracks connected and formed a large symbol encircled by smaller symbols.

I ducked as all the lights in the room shattered. Only the moon and the slight glow from the cousins' necklaces were our sources of light. When the rumbling and cracking finally stopped, Penny pressed her hand to the wall. The symbol flashed and a wave of wind whipped out, pressing us backwards.

My body tingled and my chest tightened. A slight heat emanated around my body. But it faded almost as quickly as it came on.

"WHAT THE HELL?" Addie yelled. I looked around and everyone's eyes flashed. Even my normally cool-headed mother looked ready to shift.

"Penny." Elaine noted the shift and latched onto her cousin's arm.

"That is the Liber animarum - the Book of Souls." At our confusion, Penny continued, "It's one of the ancient magical texts that harnesses the dark arts in a way to cause the most chaos and destruction. Every user of those texts went insane and killed thousands. They were supposed to have all been destroyed."

"Okay, but what's with the new decoration?" I pointed to the overly large symbol.

"It's protection runes," Elaine said. Running a hand over the markings. "Magic that is forbidden for anyone outside the Council to use. Who the hell taught you this?"

Penny looked down, refusing to answer Elaine. I rubbed my head and sighed. Every time we got close to ending this something else comes up making this even harder. It's also bringing up a few questions about Penny. Like what kind of witch was she really because that was not nature magic.

She ignored Elaine's question, instead pointing me with a look. "You coming in contact with that book is why they came here. Its magic must have rubbed off on you and when the necromancer began the spell it would have activated the residual magic. Like calls to like." Guilt bubbled. This was all because of me. My pack was dying because of me.

"This symbol will counteract any residual magic that may be here. It should also protect us from any curses she might throw at us. But—"The markings behind Penny began to glow a faint yellow just as howls broke out. "They're here." Just as the words left her mouth, loud screeching echoed through the forest.

Without a moment's thought, the men were gone. Their wolves charged through the trees. I moved to leave as well when Addie grabbed my arm. "We'll need to go to the main house. Protect the wolves there. Mum's not going to let you fight. You know that."

"I have to help, Addie. This is all my fault. I have to make this right."

She squeezed my arm. "Hey. This isn't your fault. How were you supposed to know that you were carrying traces of black magic from a grimoire? You couldn't. So, stop beating yourself up about it." I wanted to argue but she silenced me with a finger. "I'm not going to hear it. Neither will anyone else. This isn't your fault and that's that." Bossy as always. But I loved her for it.

Glancing at the carved symbol, I knew that staying put wasn't an option. Whether anyone thought it was my fault was irrelevant. The fact was, I attracted the spell, and the pack has paid the price. "Addie, I love you, but there is no way I'm going to the main house to bunker down and wait for death."

She side-eyed me. "So, you want me to convince mum to let her youngest child – who's one bite away from certain death

– stay where she can be easily targeted?" It wasn't a question. More like a statement.

"You know I'm just going to find a way to sneak out if I go," I stated matter-of-factly. "At least this way I'm not endangering anyone else beyond what I've already done."

She groaned. "Pierce, please, for once in your life just follow the rules." Her eyes were pleading with me, but I wouldn't sit on the sidelines, and she knew that.

"I need to do this, Addie."

Addie sighed. Her shoulders slumped as she accepted my decision. "This is stupid and dangerous and could get you killed." She wrapped herself around me in a tight hug. "So please, please don't die. I can't lose you."

I hugged her back and as much as I wanted to tell her that I wasn't going to die, I couldn't bring myself to lie. So instead, I said, "I promise we're going to see each other again." She gave me one last squeeze before pulling away and wiping her eyes. With a final smile, she walked to the study where my mum had gone.

It wasn't a lie. We would see each other again. But the chances of it being in this life were not high. Not with what I had planned.

Penny brushed her shoulder with mine and stared out the window as wolf and corpse clashed. "I assume we both have the same idea?" she asked in a hushed voice.

I nodded towards the kitchen where Elaine had gone. "Your cousin? Is she coming?"

"She wants to do this by the book. Rely on the council. I've left a paper with exactly what she needs to do in order to make the protection symbol. Besides, what we're going to need to do isn't going to be council approved."

I grinned. I was starting to really like thewitch.

We made our way quietly out of the house, and I silently thanked Addie for keeping my mum occupied. Outside was a harder challenge though. The forest was filled with battling wolves and prowling corpses. Without my heightened senses and with the possibility that the necromancer is focusing most of her efforts to take out Penny, this wasn't going to be easy.

In one hand I held my 9mm, gripping the handle with comfort. I was thankful that my uncle taught me how to use guns when I was younger. He was adamant that we would know how to defend ourselves beyond relying solely on our abilities. A handy ability, given my current circumstance.

On the other side of the yard closest to the trees was my car. Thankfully completely untouched. I tapped Penny's arm and we made a break for the car. We needed to be fast because all my mum would have to do was look out the window and we were done.

The car dinged and I slid into the driver's seat while Penny fell into the back with a grunt. Before I even placed the key into the ignition, the passenger door flew open. Logan's large frame piled into the car, and he slammed the door shut behind him.

I met his stormy gaze with one of disbelief. "What the hell are you doing?"

"What am I doing? What are you doing? In case you haven't noticed, we're under attack and you're one bite away from permanent death."

"Okay, this seems like a conversation we can have on the way," Penny interjected pointing to a corpse stumbling towards us. But it was missing a leg and not making much ground.

Logan looked at me daring me to argue with him further. But I only had one chance to take the necromancer down. With a loud sigh, I fired up the engine and put the car into gear. Throwing the car around, we sped down the gravel road.

Without taking my eyes off the road I asked Penny, "Can you reach in the back and see if there is anything this prick can put on?" A moment later a pair of bike shorts were thrown in between us.

"I'm not wearing this." He eyed the stretchy material with disgust.

"Quit complaining and put them on. The last thing we need is you walking around town butt naked."

"Aw, ashamed of me princess?"

"I will put a bullet between your eyes if you call me that again." I threw Penny a look in the rearview mirror as she laughed. She tried to hide her amusement by coughing. But she failed. Miserably.

CHAPTER 17

"Why are we here?" I asked Penny.

We pulled up in front of the bakery with its blown-out windows. Inside all the debris had been cleared away leaving a large barren space with only the remnants of where the counter had been.

Penny led us past the kitchen that seemed to have taken minimal damage and up a set of stairs. We walked into a small sitting room with a single L-shaped couch and a coffee table facing a fireplace bricked to the open beam ceiling. On either side were windows with the curtains open allowing moonlight to shine through the pieces of hanging crystals, bouncing light through the room.

On one side of the room were antique storage cabinets. On the other side, however, were floor to ceiling bookshelves with an array of books and little trinkets.

With a flick of her wrist, the curtain drew, and the fireplace came to life. Logan stood back, looking warily between Penny and the fireplace.

"There should be a chef's outfit in that closet that might fit you," she said to Logan pointing towards the cabinet closest to the door.

"Why are we here, Penny?" I asked again ignoring the noise Logan was making behind me. "I thought we were going after the necromancer?"

"We are, but we need a few things first."

"Like what?" Logan asked. I snorted at his outfit. I didn't realise how tight the shorts actually were on him. They fit snuggly around his round butt. But his package. Let's just say that me calling him a little dick in high school was not accurate. Along with the white coat that stretched across his biceps and hung unbuttoned, he looked like a chef stripper.

I opened my mouth to comment on his getup, but he interrupted me. "Unless you want me to work down the street naked - which I am more than happy to do - you can shut up." That little voice in my head urged me to say something wanting to call his bluff, but the look in his eyes told me he was dead serious. The worst part was, I would have liked it.

I turned my attention back to Penny just as she waved her hand in front of the books. With a click, the middle bookshelf pushed back and flipped revealing an antique mirror.

"This is so weird," Logan muttered under his breath.

"How long have you witches been in town? And has this bakery always been a witch establishment?" I asked.

"My great-grandmother moved here in her thirties setting up the bakery. Since then, there has always been a Willow witch running this place. But the majority of the staff are humans unaware of the supernatural world."

"How has no one known about your family?" Logan asked.

"Elaine and I work here on our breaks and my grandmother has a strict no magic policy while we're here. We never knew why. Until today. Plus, not everyone in the family has a strong tie to magic. Those that do go to school elsewhere and the rest either stay here or find somewhere else."

"So why are you here?" I asked. "And what kind of witch are you because there is no way you're a nature witch."

"Elaine asked me to help out while my aunt Rose was in the hospital. I figured it would be a nice relaxing break from life. And it was. Until today, obviously." Obviously. "As for your other question. I don't know."

"Huh?"

She sighed and ran a hand through her loose hair. "The Willow's are a family of nature witches. Always have been. From healers to weather witches. My mum was actually a skilled healer. But my dad's family...isn't. Their affinity lies more along with the darker arts. Not the same level as necromancy, but close enough. The problem is I don't really know where I fall and it made things difficult and tense at home. Which is why I jumped on the opportunity to come here."

There was a moment of silence as she fell into her own thoughts. Clearing her throat, she stood in front of the mirror, her necklace in hand. "Listen, in order to face the necro-mancer, I need as much access to magic as I can get. So, I'm going to need to call my familiar."

"Okay..." Logan sounded very cautious.

"Coco can be a bit of a bitch. But she won't hurt you, I promise." Logan and I shared a look. Penny placed the pen-dant on the mirror and muttered, "Veni ad me." (Come to me).

The mirror rippled and for a moment I was frozen in fear. My muscles tensed as I waited for a corpse to hurl itself through. But that didn't happen. Unfortunately.

Logan and I barely had any time to duck before a large bird flew through the mirror and over our heads at speed. It was an eagle. A large one. Coco hovered in front of the window and spread her large wings. The feathers on the underside were a deep shade of red and I knew if compared it would match the ruby in Penny's necklace.

Coco dived toward me brandishing her talons. I dropped to the floor and felt the air whoosh over my head dislodging a few hairs. She flew around the room and once again aimed for me.

"Coco!" The bird was pulled backwards suddenly by an invisible force. Penny grabbed the bird, much to her dismay, pinning her wings to her side.

"I'm so sorry!" Penny apologised. For a bird named Coco, she wasn't very sweet.

"What happened to, she won't hurt you?" I asked still sitting on the floor. I eyed the bird warily. Off to the side, Logan was doubled over laughing. I snarled at him telling him to shut up. He did but he kept that stupid smirk on his face.

"She's never done this. It might be because I've kept her locked up for a bit, but I didn't think she'd attack you." Coco let out a high-pitched whistle and Penny's eyebrows drew. "I'm so sorry. Are you okay?"

I dusted myself off. "Yeah, whatever. Now that you've got your bird can we go now?"

On the far wall next to the bookshelves was a metal cage that I had overlooked. Penny placed Coco inside and as long as she didn't spread her wings or try to fly, she would fit comfortably. With her murderous bird in hand, we left.

Logan slammed the passenger door shut and I had half a mind to deck him. Piling into the back, Penny placed the violent creature behind the passenger seat. Then she jumped back out. "Oh, I almost forgot. I'll be right back."

"Uh -" But she already took off back into the bakery.

Coco stared at me and if she was a person I'm sure she would be giving me the evil eye. Ignoring the bird, I turned the radio on and to my dismay, Logan began singing off-key.

Above, Nero squawked, looping around above us. I wound my window down and stretched my arm out for him to sit on. But he just cocked his head and flew low. The hairs on the back of my neck raised as I followed his flight path.

"What..." Logan started and then Nero diverted to the left just as a large walking corpse with half his face melting off walked under the streetlight. "Son of a bitch."

Chapter 18

My back was stiff as I aimed the gun at its head. With fingers ready to pull the trigger I took a deep breath. But I paused at the cock of its head.

"What the hell are you waiting for? Shoot the bloody thing!" Logan said. His eyes glowed as he scanned our surroundings. We were out in the middle of the street where anyone could see.

The creature lifted its hand and curled its index finger. Then it turned and slowly walked back the way it came. It was a trap, obviously. But time was not on our side, and this was faster than doing a locator spell. I met Logan's eyes across the car. He knew it as well as I did. With a loud sigh from him, we followed the creature.

We moved through the darkened streets further and further from the town centre. Thankfully we hadn't encountered anyone. But at any moment that could change. As the apartments turned to houses and more trees sprouted from the ground I realised where we were heading. Before long we reached the iron gates of St. Patrick's Cemetery. The sea of gravestones visible beyond the bars.

"A cemetery. Who could've guessed?" Logan said drily.

I reached for the lock on the gate when a whistle above sounded. Logan pulled me backwards just as Coco swooped down aiming for my hands.

"What the hell is wrong with that bird?" I asked angrily.

She landed on the brick wall and flapped her wings at me. I was going to punt the little vermin. Lucky for her, she took off before I could attempt the attack.

I made a second attempt at the lock. My fingers were inches from wrapping around the metal when a shout sounded, "Don't!" We turned just as Penny ran up to us. She pushed me out of the way and splashed a clear liquid over the lock. Smoke billowed from it and then it disintegrated into nothingness.

"It was spelled. If you had grabbed it your insides would have melted and you would have died in mere minutes." Great. That was just great.

Penny pushed the gate open with ease. Above, Coco flew ahead, her reddish tail glowing slightly under the moonlight. I was probably going to have to apologise for wanting to kill her given she did save my life.

We followed the path winding through gravestones. Eyes alert. But despite being in a prime location for an army of the dead not a single creature had been spotted. Not even the creature we followed could be sighted anywhere. I wasn't sure whether that was a good thing or not.

Further along the path, something pulled on my insides. A gentle tug. I turned in place and the pull got stronger leading towards a small white panelled church poking up behind a large tree.

"Based on how creative this witch seems to be, I'm guessing the church is where we should go," Logan said.

We moved forward quietly. The church was surrounded by well-kept grass that was littered with dry leaves and sticks. Just off the back was the caretaker's quarters, empty by the look of it. Nothing seemed out of the ordinary, but Robin once told me that witches could create illusions. The closer we moved to the church the more chills that brushed over my skin raising goosebumps.

"She's here," Penny whispered. "I can sense her magic in the air." Nerves racked my body. We were so close. My hands clenched and unclenched by my side as the adrenaline coursed in my veins.

"We need to get inside without her finding out we're here," Penny said.

Logan scoffed. "We followed a corpse that purposely led us here. She knows we're here. We may as well just go through the front."

I looked over the church and a slight semblance of a plan formed. "There are multiple entry points - the front, the back and a side one. We'll separate and take an entry point each. Logan, you'll go through the back, Penny you'll go through the side, and I'll take the front." There were no arguments from either.

Logan took off, shifting into his wolf form. Penny gave me a strained smile before tentatively walking off down the side. She would have to avoid the windows as much as possible. Although that probably didn't matter.

I pushed the front door open and was grateful when the door opened silently. That's when the normal illusion fell away. Past the tiny foyer was another set of glass-stained doors which opened to a scene from a horror movie. There were shattered windows all down the sides and the front pews had been haphazardly thrown around the room. At the front of the church, the altar was decorated with a scattering of bones and a gold bowl filled with dark red liquid. It didn't take a genius to know what that was.

To the side of the bowl was a familiar dark leather-bound book with gold foiling. The Liber Animarum. I went to grab it but pulled back when a shock coursed through my hand. Spelled. Of course. I'd have to wait for Penny. Moving my eyes from the book I looked down to where a large circle of bones and powder was bordered by symbols that had been carved into the wooden floor.

I hovered my hand over the edge of the circle and the hairs on the back of my neck stood up as a tingle washed over me. At first it started off as a cold feeling spreading through my body, but it quickly morphed into an almost overwhelming feeling of fear and dread. In a panic, I pushed myself away and the feeling abated.

Keeping as much distance as I could between myself and whatever that was, I slowly made my way through the remaining church pews. The silence was deafening. Not even the wind could be heard despite the open windows. There must have been some kind of silence spell around the building.

The creak of floorboards had my head snapping up and my .9mm cocked and ready to fire. Penny stood by a door I hadn't seen with her hands up in the air. This was the second time in one night that I'd almost shot the witch. I huffed out a breath and lowered my weapon.

"Woah," she muttered as she came around the altar. "This is some heavy stuff."

"Do you know what it is?"

She carefully manoeuvred around the circle ensuring she didn't touch anything. "I think it might be a summoning spell. But I've never seen one like this. These symbols." She pointed to each marking. "They're nothing like I've ever seen. But this setup is suggesting she's drawing an insane amount of power not just from your pack."

"And yet it still isn't enough." We whipped around and found the necromancer standing in the entryway Penny had come through. Recognition flared from two days ago. She had been one of the women in the accident at the parking lot.

Her blond hair was in a frizzy plait hanging off her shoulder. The navy-blue hood of her jacket was inches from falling off her head. Her eyes were bloodshot, and she was sickly pale with dark circles and hollowed out cheeks. She looked like the life had been sucked out of her. Like she was becoming a corpse herself.

Her eyes raked over me, surprise flaring. "You." She jaggedly moved toward me but stopped at the raising of my gun. "I can see it. His power has embedded in you. You have his mark."

She cupped her hands to her chest. Penny and I shared a look of confusion. "Have you seen him? Have you seen the great saviour himself?" Her eyes were wide and her tone maniacal. She was crazy. But I hesitated in responding. I wanted to say no, but that wasn't true, was it? I may not have seen him, but I heard him.

She must have read my expression because she laughed. It was high-pitched and unhinged. "You have! You have seen him! How was it? I bet it was wonderful! Did he say anything about me? Oh, he's going to be so happy! And you," she sneered at Penny, "will be just what I need to finish the spell. Consider it your punishment for trying to stop our good work."

Sick of hearing her voice, I lifted my gun and fired. My finger pulled the trigger over and over not pausing in its assault. I filled the necromancer with all fifteen of my bullets. Holes littered her head and chest area giving clear unobstructed views through her body to the other side.

The gun emptied and I whipped out the replacement magazine. Instead of seeing a dead body pooling with blood, the witch straightened. She turned what was left of her face to me and cackled. It was the kind of cackle that would give the wicked witch of the west a run for her money.

"How disappointing." She curled her hand in the air and I was lifted off the ground. An invisible force wrapped itself around my body and squeezed. My muscles tightened and the air in my lungs whooshed out. I struggled in the air and was sure that at any moment I would hear my spine snap.

Popping sounded in my ears and then I was suddenly dropped. I hit the floor hard and the air emptied from my lungs. I laid on the floor for a moment staring at the ceiling as I gulped in the air around me and tried to ignore the ache in my bones. Off to the side, the necromancer screamed and I turned to see Penny with her hand out toward her. Her necklace, a soft glowing red against her skin. Whatever she was doing, it was working.

I stood on unsteady feet while Penny pushed the necromancer back toward the rear of the church. Just as she passed the altar, the necromancer grabbed the bowl of blood and whipped it towards Penny. Without thinking, I jumped up and pushed Penny out of the way.

The blood splattered along my skin coating my arm and part of my face. I screamed in pure agony, falling to the floor. I clawed my skin trying to remove the blood. It was like acid eating through to my bones. My screams were all that filled my ears, echoing around the church. The pain was too much for me to handle. But just as quickly as the blinding pain came it dissipated until all I was left with was a blunt throbbing.

A numbness spread and my senses dulled. I didn't know what was happening around me. I didn't even register Penny moving me. Honestly, I don't even remember much after the pain dulled. But somehow, we ended up outside with Penny dragging me along. But the surprise was looking down and seeing my blistering arm clutching the book that started this all.

CHAPTER 19

"**S**hit, Pierce!" Logan tipped my head towards him, concern flashed in his brown eyes. "Are you okay? Is she going to be okay?"

I couldn't feel anything. Which was concerning given my charred skin, exposed nerves and the wind racing over it all. Pain is what I should have felt but the only thing I could concentrate on was how I couldn't move my arm or feel the left side of my face.

"Move." Penny pushed him out of the way and hovered her hands over the burnt side of my face. "Sana," she whispered.

Warmth emanated from her fingertips. At the sensation, my body tensed and fear pulsed as I waited for the burning to resume. Instead, a trail of tingles followed as she lightly brushed over all the burns. Quietly, she repeated the word Sana (heal), over and over again moving lower until she reached my fingertips which were still wrapped around the book.

"Is that...?" she trailed off. I uncurled my fingers as she took the book and flicked through the pages.

I flexed my hand amazed that with a single word she was able to repair the damage that in most cases was irreversible without a multitude of surgeries. It all felt normal as though I hadn't just received third-degree burns a minute ago. Magic, something I was growing more fond of by the second.

However, despite feeling normal, it didn't look normal. I trailed my eyes over the angry red skin splattered between my normal olive tone. It felt tight and slightly itchy, but I refrained from scratching. Scared I would cause more harm.

"They'll get better over the next few days," Penny assured.

"So, they'll fade into my normal skin?"

Penny pursed her lips and shook her head. "If I was a healer or you still had your healing ability, then probably. But..." But I didn't have that ability anymore. I wasn't a shapeshifter. I was human. Bitterness and anger surfaced as I stared at what would be a permanent reminder of what I was.

"Um, I think we should go," Logan said. Behind us, I could faintly hear the necromancer screaming, most likely because she realised her precious book was gone.

"No," I said. We were so close, and she had taken so much from me. There was no way I was leaving while she was still alive. "We came here to kill the bitch and that's exactly what we're going to do."

"That's not going to be easy." A high-pitched scream echoed through the cemetery chilling me to my bones. Peeking past the corner I cursed as I watched skeletal creatures claw their way up through the ground. I wondered when she was going to animate these corpses. They scurried around clearly searching for us. If they weren't running around like headless chooks, they were crawling and screeching like demons.

"No. Logan's right we need to go," Penny said. I opened my mouth to argue but she pinned me with an accusatory glare. "We are out of our depth. Especially since you left out the fact you met this great saviour, or were you planning on taking that to your grave?"

Right. I forgot about that little revelation of the necromancer's. I looked down in shame. "I'm sorry."

"How do you expect us to help if you don't tell us everything upfront? What is he? What did he look like?"

"I don't know. I didn't see him, but I heard him. When you did the locator spell, I touched you and the creature that grabbed you. Something happened and I think it built some kind of telepathic connection with him at that moment. But I haven't heard him since."

She threw her hands in the air. "Seriously! He could be in your head right now! Hell, he could be controlling you right now!"

Logan stepped in front of me, positioning himself between the two of us. "I think you should calm down," Logan said.

She closed her eyes and took a deep breath. "Okay, I'm sorry. This is all very stressful. Is there anything else I should know?"

I took a deep breath and then told her everything from the vision I had in my room to the man telling me that I was marked, and my soul would be his.

Penny was silent as she took in my information. Then she grabbed my hands in hers. "Manifesto," she whispered. There was a tug inside then coldness spread across my chest. "She was right. I don't know how we didn't pick up on it when we did the testing. You have a small trace of the same magic on the grimoire."

"What does that mean?"

"I don't know. But it can't be good. I mean, none of this is good and maybe if Elaine was here, she could tell us what this all meant." I felt so guilty. Penny was on the brink of a breakdown, and I was partially at fault. I hadn't meant to keep any of it a secret, but things came up and I just pushed it to the back of my mind. "Look, I really think we need to go back. We need backup and I need Elaine. She knows more about all of this than me. She'll tell us what to do."

In my pocket, my phone buzzed. I fished it out trying to be careful with my tender hand and silently cursed. Thirty minutes. We had thirty minutes until dawn hit. Once that sun rose people would begin waking up, moving about and heading to school and work.

This was bad, very bad. In thirty minutes the necromancer was about to have a buffet for her undead army. An influx of power. Thousands were going to die.

"I know this is a crap situation, but Penny, people are going to start waking up and going about their daily lives within an hour. We can't wait for your cousin. We're here. We need to at least try and stop her."

"Pierce, you don't understand –"

"Look, if you want to wait for Elaine that's fine. But I'm not waiting around." Penny was frustrated and scared. We all were. But time was not on our side. It was clear that she wanted to argue but finally, her shoulders slumped in defeat.

"Can you kill the necromancer," Logan asked, finally speaking after watching us. Penny thought for a second and then glancing at the grimoire she nodded. "Good. I have an idea. I'll create a distraction. Get those corpses chasing me. While I do that, you two will go into that church and finish this." He gave me a look before shifting, not waiting for a response from either of us.

Like starving animals, the corpses chased after Logan. He wound around making a run around the church ensuring he was attracting as many of them as he could. It was mesmerising watching his speed and agility as he weaved and dodged each creature that launched at him. Their teeth gnashed and shrills ripped from between their jaws. It was amazing how lifelike they could sound despite the lack of lungs and a voice box.

Penny flicked through the grimoire stopping on a page with sigils similar to the ones she put on the wall at home. The language, an altered form of English. Latin, I think. She ripped the page out and folded it into her pocket. I didn't ask and I was pretty sure she wasn't going to tell. When a clear path to the church opened, Penny and I took off. We weaved through the headstones avoiding the large holes in the grass.

Just before we made it to the church we came to a sudden stop as a creature unlike anything I had ever seen, stepped out of the shadows. It towered over us, easily over seven-foot. It cast a sinister shadow over us minus the moonlight that shone through the giant hole in between its eyes. Stitching covered its body connecting mangled pieces of flesh. A bodybuilder's arm here and a dainty hand there. The skin, a checkerboard of colours. Crudely carved symbols were an angry red under its blue and brown eyes.

Penny screamed when the creature launched itself at us. It grabbed me by my throat lifting me with its one muscled arm and dug its clawed nails into my neck. Blood riveted down my throat. I planted my shoe on its chest, my stomach rolling at the feel of soft skin. With my body somewhat stabilised I kicked up with my other. Its head snapped back with a crunch.

I scurried backwards as far as I could get clutching my neck. It stomped toward me. Its jagged mouth cut into a cruel smile. A screech from the sky had me turning in time to see Nero swooping. His talons sank into the flesh around its eyes, tearing at it to reveal white bone. The monster bucked and swiped, but Nero was faster.

With the creature focused on Nero I made my break hobbling behind a tall headstone. I sobbed at the prickling pain around my neck as my fingers tried to stop the bleeding. Behind me, the creature roared, and I shook in place. Come on, Pierce. Pull yourself together. Just breathe.

In. Out. In. Out. In. Out. I hiccupped, but slowly I calmed.

Wiping my tears, I glanced back and saw the creature trying to jump for Nero. But Nero has always been good at evading capture. I sniffled a laugh but then realised I couldn't see Penny. Where was she? I roamed my eyes over the cemetery, but I couldn't spot the witch. She must have run when the creature was trying to kill me.

I felt a pang of betrayal at that. But I couldn't blame her. She had no reason to stay, especially after all I'd kept from her. Honestly, most wouldn't have done what she and her cousin have so far. If anything, she was smart. We were going to die tonight, why should she have to?

A shadow fell over me and I looked up as Coco flew towards me. I braced for the eagle to attack, but instead, she dropped a thin metal object onto the ground. Picking it up I held the dagger and ran my hand over the red veins poking through the handle. On the very end was a rounded ruby dark in colour until you held it to light. I looked up to Coco as she spread her wings. Her eyes darted between me, the dagger and the monster.

"Will this kill it?" I whispered. She flapped her wings once and then took off toward the church. If this could kill that thing, then maybe it could also kill the necromancer.

But there was an issue. I had no bullets, one dagger and a shit-ton of undead creatures that were still being raised. There was no way I was getting into that church with that thing still there and even with the dagger, how was I supposed to get close enough to kill it?

I clenched my fist around the handle and laughed. "Come on Pierce, what's the worst that could happen? It rips me apart and the necromancer adds my body parts to that thing. Maybe she'll bring me back as an undead corpse. I'd look good as a corpse," I muttered.

The creature roared as Nero clawed at its back and to my surprise, howls answered. The dead went into a frenzy as wolves leapt over the cemetery walls. I was frozen. Wolves of all sizes engaged in a life and death battle with the roves of the dead that were still coming up through graves and out of mausoleums.

Somewhere away from me, a whistle sounded, and a small bottle flew through the air towards a group of corpses. It exploded on impact, scattering tiny pieces of bone. From the direction of the gate, Elaine walked through palming another bottle. By her side, Addie's timber wolf snarled and defended her against oncoming danger.

I smiled in relief at the sight of my sister. My knees threatened to buckle under me, but I kept upright. Across from me, Sammy strode towards me, his dark grey fur matted with chunks of things I didn't want to identify.

"What are you doing here?" I asked when he shifted and crouched by my side.

"Logan called for our help and told us what you were doing and your plan. By the way, when this is all over, I'm going to kill you after mum and dad are done with you." I choked on a sob and wrapped my arms around him. His warmth, a comfort. He gripped me tightly and I heard him sigh in relief. Like a pressure had been relieved seeing me alive.

"I can kill the witch," I told him. I lifted the dagger to give him a good look. "This can kill her and that ugly thing. But I need help."

The both of us watched as the creature charged for a wolf who thankfully got away before it wrapped its arm around them. Sammy looked back at me, and I knew he had a plan. Giving me a crooked smile, he said, "This is going to be one hell of a story in the afterlife."

Chapter 20

S ammy had filled a few of the other wolves in on our plan, including Ethan whose job was to gain the monster's full attention. In typical Ethan fashion, he charged headfirst at the creature latching onto its muscled arm. He thrashed in the air and the creature's arm started separating at the stitching.

A couple of other wolves took it as the perfect opportunity and latched onto its legs. It howled in pain and lashed out with its one free arm. Kicking its misshapen leg, it dislodged one of the wolves sending them crashing into surrounding headstones. But it didn't matter because Sammy snuck up behind it and leapt wrapping his jaw around the back of its head. The added weight threw the monster off balance and all of them went crashing down. Ethan's hind leg snapped under the monster's body and he howled in pain.

Gripping the dagger, I ran to them and jumped aiming for its heart. But it saw me, or maybe it saw the glint of steel because its multi-coloured eyes met mine mid-jump. It snapped its hand up and its fist met my tender cheek. I was thrown backwards. My back hit the corner of a headstone and I cried out as white-hot pain exploded through my whole back.

My vision blurred and black spots danced in my peripheral. I whimpered as I dragged myself to the dagger. I tried taking a deep breath to centre myself, but the pain was making it difficult. There was no doubt about it. I may not have broken my spine, but I definitely broke a couple of ribs. You would think that with the amount of pain I've been through in the last twenty-four hours I wouldn't feel anything.

After a struggle, I pulled myself up, blood dripping from the corner of my mouth. Ahead of me, Sammy was once again on the monster's back sawing back and forth dislodging skin from its shoulder. What was surprising though was the large black wolf weaving between its legs giving a bite here and there. When the creature finally dislodged Sammy, Ryker pounced going for the front of its neck sending it falling back into the destroyed lawn again.

As though they shared one mind, both men attacked simultaneously. Ryker took one arm and Sammy the other. They pulled in opposite directions and like in a movie, the light from the moon shined down illuminating my one opportunity.

Adrenaline roared through my body. Ignoring the excruciating pain, I sprinted to the creature. Sensing its impending doom, it thrashed against Sammy and Ryker, tearing its own arms from its body just as I lifted the dagger over my head and thrust down. With my entire body weight thrown behind the downward force, the sharp steel pierced through the mottled skin like butter.

The red veins in the dagger's hilt lit up and spread across the monster's chest snaking up its neck. Its eyes widened and it opened its mouth as though to scream, but only the sound of gurgling came out.

A puff of foul air and the flash of red from the ruby at the end of the hilt were all the warnings I received before the monster melted. Yeah, that's right. It melted. One second it was a squishy but solid form, the next a pile of brown sludge under my body.

That was the last straw for me. I threw myself to the side and hurled. The fluid, pinkish in colour as it mixed with my blood. When I no longer had anything left in my stomach, I dry heaved for a good minute.

Finally done, I sat on my heels and watched the fighting still happening around me. I wasn't sure where the guys had gone, probably puking themselves. While killing the monster was a win, it was a small one. All around the dead still attacked. Wolves fought in both their human and animal forms. But it was the human bodies scattered on the ground with horrific wounds that tore at my heart.

Just ahead of me a young girl lay in the grass. If you looked from the back, she appeared to be asleep. But the front told a different story. Her face was scarred by deep bite wounds and her arms bent in unnatural ways. Her brown eyes, vacant of any form of life.

Guilt threatened to choke me as it all hit me. I did this. I caused all this pain. It was because of me that families would be mourning their mothers, fathers, brothers, sisters and friends. I was the reason the pack was attacked. I was the reason they were all here at the cemetery dying.

Me.

Me.

It was all my fault.

Nero landed in front of me and squawked drawing me out of my torrent of guilt. He tipped his head and through his beady eyes I could see the blood smeared across my face mixing with tears. He cocked his head as though to ask me what was wrong, even though it was pretty clear. I was what was wrong. Me.

He chirped, hopping toward the ruby dagger. I knew what he was saying or trying to say. This was over just yet. I still had a job to finish. But I couldn't do it.

"I'm tired" I whispered. I was in pain. So. Much. Pain. My body ached and my heart felt like it was bleeding out. I couldn't do it. I couldn't finish it. "I'm sorry," I wept.

He hopped up onto my knees rubbing his beak on the back of my hand. "Let me guess, you don't want me to give up," I sniffled. He gave me a soft squawk. "How, Nero? I don't have anything left." He turned his head, and I followed his line of sight to where Addie was taking on three undead with a grace I never had.

My eyes fluttered shut as I remembered why I was doing this in the first place. Why I was even here. It was to save them, my family. I came here because she attacked us, killed our pack members and stripped half of us of our identity.

But it wouldn't have happened if you didn't attract the magic, a little voice in my head whispered. Yes, it was true, I attracted her magic, but she killed us.

Anger sparked and I grabbed a hold of it, feeding it every face I could see in the dirt, every howl of pain that sounded through the night, every scream that filled my ears and every memory of who I was before she came and tore that away.

Fire burned in my belly and rage coursed through my veins drowning out the pain. No. The necromancer wasn't winning. I came here to kill her and get revenge for all those that couldn't, and I'd be damned if I didn't.

I took the dagger in my scarred hand, wiped off the goo and stalked for the church. I wasn't coming back out unless the necromancer was dead. Come hell or high water that witch was dying today.

CHAPTER 21

I staggered into the entryway of the church, once again noting how eerily silent it was. I tucked the dagger into my pocket and scuffled my way through. As expected, the necromancer was standing at her altar the book open in front of her. What I wasn't expecting was Penny lying in the middle of the circle, her wrists slit and bleeding.

She hadn't left us. Penny's eyes were closed and her breathing shallow. Situated all around her were candles that steadily flickered with the soft breeze. She almost looked peaceful, minus the vibrant red pooling in the cracks of the wood. My eyes snapped up as the necromancer lifted her head. Her hood fell back and I froze as I met her completely black eyes. Not a single dot of white could be seen.

"It's time," she said. Her voice was discombobulated as she lifted her hands, palms facing the roof and began to chant. The flames flared and Penny groaned, her eyes blinking open.

Her eyes found mine and her fingers reached for me. "Pierce," she groaned weakly.

I ran for her, but a powerful gust of wind whipped outwards from the circle pushing me backwards. "You will not interfere," the necromancer stated. She flicked her hand out and sent me skidding backwards almost out the door.

Her chanting resumed and the wind picked up speed while the walls began to shake. The necromancer's head snapped back, and she yelled, "Occurret!" (come forward). In response, Penny's body arched, and she let out a blood-curdling scream. The flames turned green, and thunder boomed outside shaking the floor.

Penny's blood poured out of her wounds with fever. She was swimming in it. Her cries of pain were tearing me apart, my need to save her washing away all other thoughts. I lurched forward but once again I bounced against the barrier. Penny's screaming weakened just as her blood rippled and dark smoke billowed from between the bones.

In the midst of the smoke, a shape began forming. It was tall, almost the same height as the monster. Sharp bones poked out from its shoulder like armour curling towards his head. As the smoke cleared up more of its body became visible. Withered flesh was stretched over bones and glowing green orbs floated in a void where eyeballs would sit. Intricate carvings were etched all over its skull and its canines were sharpened to a point.

I took a step back and its head snapped to me. The world slowed until all I could see was those glowing green eyes piercing into my soul. He tilted his head and unhinging his jaw he screeched. My body slammed into the ground, my knees shaking at the impact. My brain was screaming for me to run but it was like my body wasn't working of its own accord.

Through my eyelashes, I watched as the necromancer fell to the ground in a bow. "It worked! I, your faithful servant, have brought you back to claim this world." Like hell he was claiming this world.

"Release me," he hissed. I paled at his whisper voice. It was him, the voice I'd heard. This was the creature that promised my soul was his. My body shook and I choked on my fear. I needed to get out. Now.

"Of course," the necromancer assured and went back to chanting. At this point, a dark mist whipped around the circle like a tornado, and the church shook as the outside elements reacted to what was happening.

With a growl, I tried to push myself up, but my muscles refused to listen. It was like I wasn't even in control of my body. I groaned as I attempted to move anything. However, that small sound was enough to get the creature's attention.

"Come to me," he commanded. His voice was like honey in my ears, and I followed his order without hesitation.

I stepped right up to the edge of the circle. He was still transparent, and I feared that once he became whole, that would be the end of everything I knew. He peered down and clicked his tongue. "Interesting. I didn't expect you to survive so long. What a pleasant surprise. Tell me, who do you belong to?"

Myself, you ugly prick. But that's not what came out of my mouth. "You. I am your servant master." The words were ripped out of my mouth as a coolness settled in my bones. I internally screamed in frustration at the realisation that he was controlling me. My body, my words, all of it, his.

He chuckled and then stretched his bone hand toward me. And like the good little servant I seemed to be, I reached back. With ease, my burned hand went past the barrier. He grabbed me, his touch a whisper on my skin but solid enough to keep my hand in place. At the contact, tendrils of dark smoke snaked across my skin. He hmphed his disapproval.

"You have something that belongs to me," he growled. "And it seems I'll have to take it back from your dead corpse." My eyes widened as a cold burning feeling raced under my skin consuming me from the inside out. Inch by inch I watched as my skin melted off my bones and I screamed. He was stripping my flesh and was going to make me watch every moment.

"STOP! Please, stop!" I sobbed. A wispy tendril wrapped around my mind and my body relaxed. No, no, no. This is wrong. Fight back, Pierce. FIGHT BACK!

There was a deep, rasping sound and then something sharp latched into my neck. For a split second his control on my body slipped, but that was all I needed. I ripped myself backwards, out of his grip and away from the circle. The smoke slammed into the barrier trying to reach me, but he was contained.

Looking down I whimpered at the patches of sinew and cream bone visible on my hand. What did he do to me? The only good thing was that I couldn't feel it. But that might have been because of nerve damage more than anything else. If I managed to survive this night there was a strong possibility I was going to have to amputate this arm.

There was a scream and the flames started flickering. Behind the circle, the necromancer crouched covering her head as Nero swooped, attacking her with his talons. I ran my fingers over the back of my neck and there I felt three holes that I knew would match his talons.

"Finish the spell!" The creature bellowed slamming against the barrier and that's when I saw Penny, still lying on the floor. She was sickly pale, and I knew beyond a shadow of a doubt that she was the sacrifice. The stronger and more solid he became, the closer to death she got.

I racked my brain, trying to work out how to get out of this situation. I couldn't just grab Penny. The second I made it past the barrier he was going to grab me, and I'd be a pile of bones. Killing her would ensure the spell wouldn't work but

I couldn't kill her. She had done so much for us. No, I had to save her. There had to be something. I ran my hand down my pants and felt the cool metal of the dagger still in my pocket, waiting. All I needed was the perfect opportunity.

But then it happened.

I watched the scene in front of me like I was in a movie. Nero was flying around the room taking a shot here and there at the necromancer. But it was a single moment, where she latched her eyes on him and flicked her finger up, yelling, "MORI!" (die).

"No!" I screamed as a stream of magic slammed into Nero. Everything slowed as I watched Nero's small black feathered body drop from the air smacking into the floor with a sickening thud. Wings outstretched with feathers scattered all around him and a tiny splattering of blood near his beak. His normally mischievous eyes were dull. There was nothing staring back.

Dead. Nero was dead.

I screamed out in anger and pain, my vision swimming with red. Nothing else mattered as I zeroed in on the witch. I palmed the dagger and with raw rage, I threw it. The steel twinkled through the air reflecting the green of the flames. It flew true and straight through the partially transparent creature. The tip pierced the necromancer's skin, and the momentum of the throw pushed the dagger forward until the handle touched her neck.

A cold grin spread across my face as she choked and her eyes widened, the black seeping out to reveal pale irises. Gripping the handle, she tried to dislodge the dagger, but it didn't budge. Red lines snaked over her body and anticipation built as I waited for her gruesome death. Blood spurted out of every hole in her face like a fountain and she violently shook. Her body stopped suddenly before she fell to the floor, her skin sinking into itself.

The monster roared in anger. Snarling, he launched for me, but the ground shook and the dagger filled the room with a bright red light. My head snapped back and blunt force hit me square in the chest and dug into my skin. Magic spread throughout and my senses fluctuated.

The feeling abated just in time for me to see the creature pull himself to his full height, the mist wrapping itself around his body. "You will pay for that!" he roared. He flexed his fingers and that cold burning feeling started around my collar again. But a power more vicious and wild rose in challenge. My lips pulled back and a deep, animalistic snarl answered him.

"Impossible," he whispered. I didn't know what was happening, but my eyes sharpened and the dark room became clear as day. Looking at the creature, I could see the dark magic coalescing around him, but it was the red flame that caught my attention.

Behind, Penny stood on wobbly legs. Her face was still pale but there was a fire-like light swirling around her. Tendrils of the light branched out and the green flames turned orange. With a flick of her wrist, the sigils and bones were scorched.

The creature turned on her and snarled, "You think you can kill me? You are nothing compared to me! You can't kill me!"

"No," Penny wheezed. "But I can send you back to the shit-hole you came from."

She stretched out her hand and the flames burst from the candles encircling both into an infinity symbol. Her palms were upturned and floating in front of her was the paper that she had ripped out earlier.

"No!" it screamed. Blood began pouring down Penny's arm and out of her nose, but she remained strong, her face a mask of determination. The fire wavered slightly, and the creature laughed, "You're not strong enough to send me back, witch." But Penny ignored him.

There was a high-pitched whistle and in flew Coco her red feathers brightly lit as if she was on fire. Penny's hand reached above her head, and she grasped Coco's feet, the eagle spreading its large wings to its full length. Together, Coco and Penny's magic flared, and I covered my head just as a bright light exploded all around searing the back of my eyes.

When I opened my eyes symbols floated from the flames and pulsated in the air.

Once.

Twice.

The third time was quickly followed by a wave of energy slamming through everything, including me. My head cracked against the leg of a church pew and darkness consumed my vision.

Chapter 22

The blackness faded becoming little spots on the edge of my vision. Blinking away the blurriness I attempted to move but I whimpered at the stabbing, throbbing pain. My head felt way too tight, constricting to the point of being painful. Nausea clawed its way up my throat. But thankfully being on my back made it difficult for anything to come up. I didn't even think anything would come up considering I had emptied my stomach earlier.

Blinking slowly, I fought against the darkness that threatened to drag me down to its depth. I felt drowsy and I suddenly just wanted to sleep. But I had enough sense to know that if I gave in, I was never waking up.

Just above me, tiny grey particles swam in the air. Leisurely making their descent. I tried to inhale but all I managed to do was choke. Droplets of liquid splattered my face as I coughed. The tightness in my chest was getting worse and I realised a large piece of the roof was on top of me. Tears flowed freely and every small breath filled my sinuses with ash and dust, worsening the pain. I was in agony and slowly I was being crushed while also choking on what I could safely assume was my blood. What a horrible way to die.

I slowly turned my head and was met with the roof crumbled all over the floor, caving some parts of the floor in. But amid the rubble, there was a pale hand poking out coated in dust and blood.

"Penny," I called weakly, my voice raspy. Please don't be dead. Please, please, please don't be dead. "Penny," I called again, but there was no answer. She needed help. I needed to help her. But my head was throbbing so bad, that the slightest movement made me feel sick.

There was a grunt and then the heavy weight on my chest was lifted off. My lungs tried to draw in air, but I just coughed up more blood. Out from the side, Sammy's face filled my vision and I wanted to cry out in relief at the sight of my brother. His chest was coated in mud, blood and scratches that went jaggedly through the dragon tattooed across his shoulder and chest. His mouth moved but no sound came out or maybe I just couldn't hear him. He gripped my body and attempted to pull me up, but I moaned in pain.

"I'm so sorry," Sammy said as my hearing came back. His eyes scanned my body and I could see the panic set in as he took in all my injuries. He hovered over me; forehead pressed against mine. "You're going to be okay. You hear me, Pierce? You're going to be fine. You're going to be fine." Not sure whether he was trying to convince me or him. But his words sent an ache through my chest.

I tried to tell him that it was okay, but only incoherent sounds came out. He turned around yelling at someone, but my hearing kept fading in and out. With more effort than it should have been, I skimmed my fingers over his chest drawing his attention back to me. I was struck by the pure fear that swam in his steel blue eyes.

"Penny," I whispered.

"We'll get her out. Just worry about yourself, okay." I wanted to know if she was okay, if she was alive, but nothing came out. Instead, I opened and closed my mouth like a fish gasping for water.

The rattle of my chest had Sammy yelling for someone to come quick. But I didn't think they were going to be quick enough. In the back of my mind, I could feel death beckoning me, but I wasn't done yet. There was so much I needed to know. So many questions still swimming in my mind. I wanted to ask him if it was gone. Did Penny do it? Did she send that creature back to where it came from? Was the necromancer really dead? Was it over? Were we safe?

Sammy must have seen the questions in my eyes because he nodded his head. "You did it, Pierce. You saved us."

The words took a little time to register, but when they did, I smiled. Happiness and relief washed over me, making everything worth it. All the pain that I've endured, worth it. More tears fell but this time they were happy ones.

We did it. We actually won. We saved the pack. The town. We did it.

My blinking slowed as tiredness pulled at me, my limbs feeling heavy. Sammy tried to say more but my consciousness began to fade, blinking in and out. But I knew without hearing him that he was pleading with me to stay. To hang on a little longer, but I could only keep death at bay for so long. My injuries were bad, and I knew I wasn't going to last long.

Addie came into view on my other side, her normally neat hair was frizzed, and tears poured down her muddied cheeks. She gripped my face gently in her hands, her face one of hysteria. I weakly gripped her hand, and I could feel the sobs wracking her body.

I wanted to tell her - tell them both - that everything was going to be okay and that they didn't need to worry. I finished what I set out to do. What better way to die than knowing they were safe? My mother and father, Sammy, Addie, Robin, the pack, the town, all of them alive and safe.

Safe.

My heart slowed and it felt like weights had been put on my eyelids. Above me, the light from the dawn pierced through the sky filling it with pinks, yellows and oranges that chased the night away. A beautiful end to a horrific night in my opinion.

I blinked once and slowly exhaled. A howl long and as clear as the sky above called to me, beckoning me. So, I followed.

EPILOGUE

4 months later.

The bitter liquid slid down my throat as condensation dripped onto my cheek. It was shit, but then again, I didn't exactly pay for the good stuff. I huffed as I eyed the clear bottle of vodka teasing me from behind the bar. It was practically calling my name.

"You good, mate?" I looked the older bartender up and down and a growl threatened to slip out. All I wanted was to be left alone, but he hadn't done me wrong. It wasn't his fault that he picked this shitty town to live in. Well, technically it was.

"Fine," I replied through clenched teeth. He raised his bushy grey eyebrow but didn't press. Smart move.

I swallowed the rest of the beer slamming it down on the counter harder than I intended. Thankfully though, it didn't shatter. I doubt the bartender would have taken kindly to that and I would hate to have to pummel his face in.

At the thought of violence, my wolf raised its head, and I gritted my teeth as I attempted to keep him in check. Bloody thing has been aching for a fight nightly. Normally, I would indulge him, but not here. Not in this town.

I made my way outside and just my luck it was raining, and I didn't have my car. I had decided that going for a run to the bar was the better option. Groaning I made my way down the street lit by street lights and storefronts still operating. It was around six or maybe seven. I honestly didn't know how long I had been sitting on that stool drinking. All I know was that it wasn't anywhere near long enough to get me drunk. Around me, people bustled around going about their nightly activities. It was more active than the last time I was here. Then again, I spent most of my time in the woods and only saw this place in the early hours of the morning.

A woman much shorter than me shouldered me as she walked past chatting animatedly with her friend. I went to snarl at the contact but stopped when her innocent brown eyes looked up at me and for a moment, I was frozen as I pictured another with her wolf-cut hair and permanent glare always aimed at me. But the woman's soft sorry snapped me out of my vision and I watched as she and her friend scurried off. I raked my hand through my overgrown hair. I really hated it here.

My phone buzzed in my pocket. Pulling it out I sighed at the caller I.D. "Cousin!" I greeted cheerily.

"Where are you?" Ryker asked in a gruff voice.

"Oh, you know, just enjoying everything this incredible town has to offer," I replied, sarcasm dripping from every word.

He snarled and both my wolf and I flinched. "Are you drunk?"

I rolled my eyes. "No." Unfortunately.

"Good. We're heading out in ten. Be back before then or run home." His tone was short and left no room for argument. Not that I would. Putting this town behind me was at the top of my list of priorities. But I had a feeling I knew why he was being so cranky.

"She won't come back huh." I took his silence as confirmation. Ryker had come up with some crap story about coming here to make sure that the people we were hunting weren't hiding out somewhere here or close by. But they weren't. In fact, we had tracked them closer to the city. No, he came back for Addie.

After a beat, I asked in all seriousness, "Is she okay?"

He scoffed. "About as okay as you are. Even worse actually. None of them are okay." And who could blame them? It had been four months since the necromancer's attack on the Parsons' pack. The remnants of what happened those two days were still felt by all. Many had died that day, including Pierce.

The memory of that morning surfaced without warning, and I had little time to brace myself. I had just helped realign the arm of a wolf when I heard Addie screaming. When I got to the church Ryker was holding a hysterical Addie as she fought against him, wailing for Pierce. My stomach had dropped and that's when I saw Samuel bent over a smaller body. His cries stabbed my heart as I realised what had happened. His second, Ethan, and a few others had finally pulled him away from her and that's when I collapsed.

I'll never forget seeing her laying on the floor caked in blood and her burn marks visible along the left side of her body. It was like I had been hit by a truck and then dragged through glass as I stared at Pierce – beautiful, fierce, Pierce, who was lying dead with wounds more horrific than I had ever seen.

I threw myself down an alleyway as the memories forced me into a crouching position. Bile threatened to rise as I remembered seeing her bones where her skin had fallen off. Apparently, we could thank whatever fucked up thing the necromancer had tried to raise for those wounds. For weeks after the only thing I could think about day in and day out was the fact that she was dead. Pierce Parsons was dead.

From in my hand, Ryker's voice broke through the haze bringing me back into the present. "She can't leave. Not yet at least. I'm going to give her until after we've dealt with this situation."

"And then what?" I asked, grateful for the distraction. "It's not like her pack would just let you kidnap her."

"She's to be my wife. She can't stay here."

"Ryker, her sister died along with numerous others in her pack. Four months isn't enough, especially with how close they were. If you force her hand before she's ready the two of you will be back to square one. Hell, they may even call off the union, screw the consequences." He growled in response, but he knew I was right.

"You've now got eight minutes." And with that, he hung up.

I huffed at his pushiness, but I was glad for the distraction from the memories. The sooner he and Addie got back on good terms, the better it would be for me. He's been more invested in what I do and don't do, and it's been pissing me off.

Finally, making it into the woods, I shifted with little care for my clothes which ripped as my wolf broke free. I shook my fur and I inhaled the crisp air and all the scents that came with it. Behind I could scent the various foods and ahead I could pinpoint where a couple of kangaroos were still milling about.

I relished the feeling of my muscles sprinting me faster than my human form ever could. The wind raked through my fur. It was honestly a feeling like no other running in my wolf form. As I closed in on the Parsons compound the wind shifted and an unknown scent caught my attention. I skidded to a stop, my eyes scanning my surroundings. The wind blew again and there on the current was the scent of something supernatural, but it wasn't clear what.

I took off after, following the scent until I came up to a cliff overlooking the vastness of the woods. Standing on the very edge was a large wolf with its back to me. From this distance, I could get a better scent, but it only confused me more. It was a wolf, yet not. My hackles raised and I crouched ready to attack. Then it turned.

My eyes met a bright amber eye surrounded by almost black fur, but the other eye was milky white. The fur down the left side was a lighter brown dispersed amongst the darker fur. But it was the fur hanging over pockets of bones covered in thin withered skin that stopped me.

It was a beast. One that shouldn't exist. Yet the longer I stood here the more there was something almost familiar about it. It snarled at me, and a chill broke out at the haunting almost demonic sound that skated over my body shaking me to my core. I wanted to run, but I was frozen in place.

With a snort, it turned and then jumped. That snapped me out of it. I ran to the edge and looked over expecting to see a large body broken on the cliff's edge or splattered onto the forest floor, but there was nothing. I scanned the trees, but still there was nothing, Impossible.

Then I heard it. A howl chilling to the bone. It wasn't a call. More like an announcement. I shivered. I really did hate this town.

www.ingramcontent.com/pod-product-compliance
Lightning Source LLC
Chambersburg PA
CBHW071019180726
48291CB00004B/1544